Delsie

Joan Smith

LARGE PRINT

Oxford

First published in Great Britain 2007
by
Robert Hale Limited

Published in Large Print 2008 by ISIS Publishing Ltd.,
7 Centremead, Osney Mead, Oxford OX2 0ES
by arrangement with
Robert Hale Limited

British Library Cataloguing in Publication Data
Smith, Joan 1938–
   Delsie. – Large print ed.
   1. Widows – Fiction
   2. Aristocracy (Social class) – Fiction
   3. Love stories
   4. Large type books
   I. Title
   813.5'4 [F]

         ISBN 978–0–7531–8066–2 (hb)
         ISBN 978–0–7531–8067–9 (pb)

                20224405
   Printed and bound in Great Britain by
   T. J. International Ltd., Padstow, Cornwall

Delsie

CHAPTER ONE

The day that was to mark the beginning of the change in Delsie Sommer's life began like any other. The sun did not shine more brightly; she awoke with no tingling feeling of excitement, no presentiment at all that her life was to be turned topsy-turvy, that danger and excitement and romance were awaiting her around the corner. No, she awoke with a slight nagging headache at seven o'clock, dragged herself out of bed to light the fire and put on water for tea, dressed hurriedly in her well-worn navy bombazine gown, and twisted her dark hair into its required knot, like a spinster. She gulped her tea, bread, and cheese in the austere but tidy apartment on the third floor of Miss Frisk's genteel rooming house. On went the winter pelisse and dark bonnet even if it wasn't quite winter yet, because the sky was gray and there was sure to be rain before she got home. Silently down the stairs to the second storey — back up to get the notebooks she invariably forgot. It was some unconscious rejection of the role of schoolmistress, she supposed, that accounted for this habitual forgetting of the students' books. She wished she could set fire to them all and throw Mr Umpton, the principal, on top of the blaze.

She smiled as she imagined the toes of his boots smoldering, smoking, finally bursting into flames. Would that, at last, make it warm enough for him? His habitual complaint, "My, but it's cold in here," as he rubbed his hands together every morning, went through her head like a song as she hurried along the shaded lane to St Mary's Parish School. My, but it *was* getting cold, though! A real winter nip in the air, and here it was just beginning November. Whose stupid idea had it been to place the village school half a mile beyond the edge of the village? She supposed they got the lot two pounds cheaper, and never mind that all the students and two teachers had to walk in wind and snow and rain. Or was it Mr Umpton's idea, that the parents not see what an inordinate fraction of the day his pupils "took a breath of air" outside when they should be doing their work?

"What odds?" he said one day to Delsie, and had regretted a dozen times since. "A little reading, a little writing, a few sums; and the kings and queens of England, and there you have more knowledge than most of their heads can hold, or will ever use." The fact of the matter was, it was about as much knowledge as he had to impart, yet he insisted on taking the older class himself — for the prestige of it, she supposed. The students knew those bare facts and a few more before Mr Umpton got hold of them. "Consolidation, there's the thing," he told her, when she pointed out to him that his class had already been through the Second Reader. "Let 'em consolidate what little they've

2

learned. Better to know a little bit well than to have a glimmering of a lot that's above their heads."

The handful of bright ones who grew tired of consolidating either left in despair or came to Delsie after classes to push on to the Third Reader and start fractions. But there weren't really many who cared for learning. Most of them were there because the school was free and their parents made them go, and of course it was easier than picking stones from the fields for the roads, or helping their fathers on the farms. Subtle hints dropped to Mr Umpton that she would be happy to exchange classes with him — "privately, just between the two of us. There is no need to tell the Board" — were met with a jealous eye and a harsh tongue.

"If you're not happy at St Mary's, Miss Sommers, it can be arranged for you to be replaced," he said. And Mr Umpton was the very one to arrange it, the brother-in-law of the director.

"Oh, no, I am quite happy," she said, and had not raised the question again. She needed the job.

Life had been hard for Delsie. Born aboard a ship returning from the West Indies, she felt she had been adrift ever since. Her mother was from a branch of a noble tree, but on a rather lower tip of it, amounting almost to a twig. When she married Papa, a younger son of a genteel family, they had gone off to the West Indies with barely enough money between them to get there and set up house. Papa had magnificent ideas. Had he started with ten thousand pounds, he might possibly have made a million. But, starting with one thousand, he had overreached himself and lost what he

3

had to his creditors. Ambergris was the villain that had done him in, something that came from whales, Mama said, and was used in making perfume. Her mother's family had bailed them out and brought them back to England. It was on that journey that Delsie had been born. Papa had next tried his hand at being a solicitor, and failed less gloriously than with ambergris. Again money was wangled from Mama's family, for horse breeding in Ireland this time, and again it was a failure. Papa had died in Ireland, and it was back home to England again, but the family's patience was wearing thin. One hundred and fifty pounds a year for the widow was all they could see their way clear to give. It was barely enough to live on.

The family possessions were sold off bit by bit — first silver, then portraits, finally the pearls and a pair of rings, to give Delsie the lady's education her mama insisted on — four years at a seminary in Bath as a day student, while living in rented rooms with Mama. All this sacrifice was to make Delsie eligible to contract a good match, but how was anything of the sort possible without a penny of dowry?

"We have better blood than any of them, if it comes to that!" Mama used to say, clutching a worn shawl about her shoulders — but a cashmere shawl, once good — to keep out the drafts. "My great uncle Foster is a marquess — the Marquess of Strothingham. If I applied to *him* we should not be living as we are."

"Perhaps you should do so, Mama," Delsie suggested, more than once.

4

"Yes, and perhaps I *shall* one of these days," was the invariable answer. But she never did, being as proud as a peacock. It was Papa who had groveled to the relatives. Later Delsie read that the Marquess of Strothingham had died at seventy-eight of a heart attack, leaving a vastly encumbered estate to some nephew. Delsie hadn't the heart to tell her mother. Uncle Foster was a symbol; she had come to realize that over the years. The name of the heir was mentioned casually in another conversation, and Mama had never heard of him. When she was eighteen, her mother too had died. It was a peaceful passing — a year's gradual subsiding into listlessness, a month in bed, eating next to nothing. The local doctor said she had fluid in the liver. It was the most common complaint in town, the one accused in all deaths whose cause the man did not know.

Miss Sommers found herself alone in the world, with Mama's allowance cut off, no known family (for they never visited the relations, nor was any acknowledgment of the death notice returned), and nowhere to go. She had her lady's education, so painfully acquired, with no pianoforte to play, no dining room in which to serve dinners, no friend to whom she might speak her French, not even a set of water colors to paint the wild flowers she loved.

A job, then, she said to herself, and discovered a streak of practicality she hadn't known she possessed. After perusing the newspapers, she answered three advertisements for a governess, had an offer from two, and accepted the first. For two happyish years she had been governess, half nursemaid really, to two rosycheeked young daughters of a successful leather merchant in Bath.

The Johnsons were kind to her, and, though she was not treated as a daughter, she was treated well. Then Mrs Johnson's sister came to them for Mrs Johnson's third lying-in. The mother and child survived but the peace of the household did not. The sister took Delsie in jealous dislike and made her life so miserable that she left before she was turned off. With her new practicality, she had a new position lined up before leaving. Back home at Questnow, St Mary's Parish School was looking for a teacher. They advertised for a male, but Delsie answered it and, with a little help from the vicar, got the job. Her modest salary of a hundred pounds a year may have been instrumental. A male would have got half as much again.

So it was back to Questnow, the sleepy little village by the sea that she and her mother had ended up in after returning from Ireland so long ago, and where they had lived till the remove to Bath for schooling. It was originally the name that had attracted them.

"We are on a quest now, Delsie, a quest for peace and happiness. I hope we may find it here. I love the sea. You, who were born at sea, must like it too." They had found relative peace, but little true happiness.

How happy could a young girl be, constantly reminded of her gentility, constantly urged not to associate with the other children on the street, daughters of fishermen and chandlers and even smugglers? No, it had not been happy, looking through

6

a window at youngsters having a good time playing with a ball or a rope, while one must herself be content with an infinitesimally small back yard, or a parlor. As she grew older, she came to realize happiness for her mother and herself lay further up the coast, on a promontory that was called simply deVigne's hill. There was the Olympian world of gentility, even nobility, for the owner of the hill and all that lay within its ken was Baron deVigne, sixth baron and holder of the domain. When he rode into Questnow in his crested carriage, or astride his high-bred mount, or in one of his fancy sporting curricles, every eye turned. The common folk, most of whom were beholden to him in one way or another — either as a tenant, or with a son or daughter in his employ, or the recipient of outright charity — bobbed their heads in respect as he passed. Delsie Sommers never curtsied. Neither she nor her mother owed anything to him.

"Our blood is as good as his," Mama said, but in a defensive way. The blood may have been, but there equality ended. The house, the carriages, the clothing, even the face and form of the deVigne line — all were unexceptionable. The baron himself was tall, well-formed, dark and handsome, with only a slightly arrogant cast to his countenance to mar perfection. The sundry ladies who accompanied him to the village in his carriage were also objects of keen interest. Whether dowager, daughter, friend, or relative, they all seemed to possess elegance, and if not actually beautiful, there was an aura of glamor surrounding them that was stronger than mere beauty. Their lovely bonnets, their exquisite gowns, their tinkling silver laughter, breathed of money, of a life of ease and refinement. They came to Questnow, sometimes in groups, sometimes singly, sometimes with children, often with dogs, but always bringing with them that whiff of glamor and excitement, and invariably leaving in their wake a fierce sense of resentment in the heart of Delsie Sommers. These people became known by sight to Delsie and her mother as deVigne's aunt, Lady Jane, who had a husband called Sir Harold, the pair of them living in the Dower House on the hill. There was deVigne's sister, Louise, who was married to a Mr Grayshott, a fabulously rich commoner. This pair were not seen much except in the summer, when they inhabited a structure, also on the hill, called simply Grayshott's cottage. The old Dowager Lady deVigne passed away early on. Each new beauty that accompanied deVigne to town was examined with curiosity, always with the thought that she might eventually be the new Lady deVigne, a post as yet unfilled.

Delsie used to imagine what it would be like to live up there, on the hill, in one of the fabulous mansions that dotted the slope. There would be parties, frequent company, horses, trips to London, fine rooms, and parks and gardens. The Hall, Baron deVigne's own' establishment, was said to have more than forty chambers abovestairs. It was surely criminal for one man to have so much space to himself, when she and her mother must be cramped into three small rooms.

"Strothingham's Abbey has *fifty* bedrooms," Mama said. Much good they did the Sommerses!

The years dragged by slowly in Questnow. Delsie grew from a child to a young lady and finally went away to Bath, with never a sign of recognition from the deVignes. They were too poor, and their rich blood too unknown, to be on calling terms with the local nobility, yet not poor enough to excite charity. They inhabited a sort of anonymous no-man's-land, meeting only occasionally in the village streets or being in the same building at church on Sunday. The deVignes did not attend the local assemblies, and the Sommers ladies held themselves above going to deVigne's annual public day to rub shoulders with tenant farmers and fishermen. There was no common meeting place, and so through the years they never met.

Though they were not formally acquainted, one of the gentlemen on the hill became aware of the quiet young lady who did not curtsy to deVigne, who looked past them all with a nonchalant gaze which successfully concealed her rampant interest in them and all their doings. He became first aware, then interested, and finally infatuated to an almost insane degree.

Delsie did not hear, while at Bath, that Mrs Grayshott had died in childbirth. When she returned to Questnow after graduation, Mr Grayshott was already a widower of one year, and, Miss Sommers had blossomed into a handsome, accomplished young lady with a pair of clear, imperious gray eyes, a strong chin, a lofty bearing, and a crown of chestnut curls. He made any excuse into the village to see her, spent whole mornings lounging outside the local inn, just to catch a glimpse of her as she went to the post office or to the shops. Finally, the week after Mama's death, he came to call.

In her gratification at seeing Mr Grayshott, brother-in-law to deVigne, at her door, Miss Frisk lost her head and had Delsie called down to her own parlor to meet him. Mr Grayshott had a young daughter — he was clearly come to offer Miss Sommers the job of tending her. What a blessing for the girl! Her mama just dead, and money certainly in very short supply. Delsie spoke of looking for a position. Though she never learned the truth of that meeting, she could not have been more surprised than Miss Sommers herself at what transpired.

Upon first entering the parlor, Delsie had recognized Mr Grayshott. His general contours, his outfit, were familiar, as one knows by sight a familiar landmark, yet on closer examination she found the face to be not as she expected. Older, for one thing, more lined, the eyes fatigued and the mouth having a despondent downward curl to the lips. Ah, but Miss Frisk had mentioned his losing his wife — that would account for it. Before long, she also discerned something unmentioned by Miss Frisk. Mr Grayshott had been drinking. The aroma, and a certain unsteadiness in both speech and legs, told this as clearly as if he held a bottle in his hands. "Forgive my coming here, unknown to you," he said, bowing formally. "I am Grayshott. I live up on the hill." He waved a hand vaguely towards the north.

"How do you do, Mr Grayshott. I take it you are aware who I am, as you have asked to see me." Her conclusion as to his asking to see her coincided exactly with Miss Frisk's. She had been elated at first. What an excellent thing to have a good job land in her lap, one as well that would take her up the hill. When she realized he had been drinking, she wondered if it were a regular thing with him, in which case she was loath to go to work for him.

"Does not all the world know Miss Sommers?" he asked, his voice becoming wild.

"I shouldn't think so," she replied, in confusion.

"Modest! Oh, too modest. You must know I have been admiring you from afar."

"Indeed, Mr Grayshott!" She looked at him in alarm, eyeing the door in case of requiring a hasty exit.

"Forgive me! My emotions overpower me, seeing you like this for the first time. So lovely, lovelier even than I had supposed. Since the death of your poor mother, I have begun to hope — only hope, Miss Sommers — I do not by any means take it for granted . . ." He stopped, weaving on his feet, and a foolish smile settled on his hagged features as he sank into observing her.

She arose and edged towards the door. "What is it you want of me?" she asked, deciding on the spot she would refuse the position he had come to offer.

"I want you to be my wife."

"Oh!" She stared in blank astonishment. "You cannot be serious!"

"I am totally serious. Marry me, Miss Sommers, and I will do all in my power to make you happy. I have loved you ever since your return to Questnow. I could not believe, when I heard in the village, that you were the little girl who left some years ago to go to school. Do not fear this is only a passing fancy."

"It is quite impossible!" she replied, becoming angry at his impertinence.

"Make it possible! Say yes," he implored, his voice becoming maudlin.

"I'm sorry. No, I could not possibly." She reached the door and fled upstairs to her room, without even saying good-bye. She was trembling from head to foot when she sat on the edge of her bed, as if she had just escaped a horrible fate. She marveled at the strange interview for days, but it was just at this time that she received the offer from the Johnsons, and her life was busy arranging the move, so that she did not dwell on it as she might otherwise have done. It became, in time, a bizarre experience she could consider with amusement — the day poor Mr Grayshott had come to her, drunk, and offered marriage.

When she returned to Questnow again after leaving the Johnsons, to take up her post at St Mary's School, she rather wondered if Mr Grayshott would repeat his solicitation. Meeting him on the street one day a week after her return, she observed that he had gone rapidly downhill. His drunkenness was apparent now at a glance. His clothing had become disheveled, his hair not well groomed, and his face not lately shaved. He presented an altogether displeasing appearance. She crossed the street to avoid meeting him head on. But her tactic was in vain. Again he came to her at Miss Frisk's, to which apartment she had returned, and again he made his preposterous offer, in more exaggerated phrases than formerly. And again he received very short shrift.

"Please go away and don't bother me again," she said coldly. She was older now, more sure of herself, and he was no longer a character of any importance. She gave it very little thought this time.

He had not bothered her again. He cast soulful eyes at her when they passed occasionally on the streets of the village, but he did not approach her, and after a few months she ceased to see him. Then her life settled into a dull routine, teaching at the school, reading in the evening, or playing piquet with Miss Frisk, who was making a bosom bow of her, going occasionally to a villager's home for an evening of entertainment, as she would not have been allowed to do had Mama been alive. But a young girl needed some company after all, and so she went.

On that dreary morning in early November, she plodded along the road to the school, with no thought that before she had returned to her room a whole new horizon would have opened before her. There would be a crack in the magic door that would lead eventually to the hill.

CHAPTER
TWO

Baron deVigne sat in the morning parlor at the Hall in a deep concentration, staring with unseeing eyes through the French doors to the autumnal remains of a rose garden, with an occasional glance beyond to see if Lady Jane was approaching yet. He had a fair idea why she wanted to see him. After a little while he saw her tall, gaunt figure, wrapped up in a huge cape of gentian violet, trundling along the footpath from the Dower House, her head bent. Poor old girl, she's getting on, he thought. It was with solicitude that he welcomed her, took her shawl, and ordered her a glass of sherry.

Her sagging cheeks waggled in pleasure as she took the glass. She had gray hair, a beaklike nose that always turned red in the cold, and a pair of mischievous blue eyes that lent an air of youth to her lined face. "Just what I need," she told him in her deep voice, and knocked the sherry off at a gulp, holding out her glass for a refill. "Good stuff. Now, down to business. Tell me, Max, what is to be done about it?"

This cryptic question was apparently clear to deVigne. "Something must be done at once. He was foxed again last night. That Miss Milne you hired to look after Roberta came dashing over here at nine o'clock close to hysterics, and the silly chit hadn't even the sense to bring Bobbie with her. She left the child there, in the house with a drunken father. I went over and got her, of course. They are here now in the schoolroom, the pair of them. I don't mean to let Roberta go back to that house. With Grayshott drunk three quarters of the time, it is no place for his daughter. God only knows what he might do — set the place ablaze one night and have them all burned to a crisp. Miss Milne, too, has begun dropping hints she means to leave, and who shall blame her?"

"Dear me, what a fix. It begins to look as though we must have him put away at last. He has become a confirmed alcoholic. The courts surely will support our claim."

"They will agree to remove her from *his* charge, but it is his uncle, you know, who will be her guardian. I cannot like to see my sister's daughter remove to Clancy Grayshott's establishment, where she will be exposed to horse dealers, smugglers, and worse. That is no place for a deVigne to be raised, when there are our two houses eager to have her."

"It would be no worse than staying with her father, at least."

"It would be better, but not good enough. A dirty set of dishes we have got connected with through Louise's marriage. When I helped Samson put Grayshott to bed last night, I was appalled at his condition. A room full of medication. I spoke to Samson about him, and he feels, from what the doctor says, that Grayshott hasn't long to live. In his will, you know, he puts Roberta in

Clancy's charge. Spite. All spite because of the way Louise's marriage portion was tied up in the child. He wants to get his hands on it and squander it as he did his own money. Ran through a handsome fortune in the space of three years. And because I refuse to comply, he has made Clancy the guardian in spite. Clancy has hated us forever. We'll never be allowed to even see Roberta. I am at my wits' end trying to sort this muddle out."

"Poor Louise. If only she had lived, things would have been fine. Grayshott only became a loony after her death. He was crazy about her. He has those uncontrollable emotions. The right woman could have done anything with him. It's a great pity that young schoolteacher could not have seen her way clear to accepting him."

"Do you think he actually offered for her? I remember he used to run on about her soulful eyes."

"According to local gossip, he offered more than once and was roundly snubbed both times. I was sorry to hear at the time that he was interested in her, but I have often regretted since that time that she refused. One cannot but wonder why she did. Scratching for a living. You'd think even Grayshott would be better than teaching at the parish school. And she is the soul of propriety — would have kept him in line, or I miss my bet."

"Yes, it is a pity, but what is to be done?"

"Do you think it is too late for her to have him yet? She's had a year of pitting herself against those rowdy

16

students. I wonder if she wouldn't take him now, where she turned him off before."

"He's gone straight downhill the last year. If she refused him when he was relatively sober, I cannot think she'll marry a drunkard."

"If he hasn't long to live, as the doctor thinks . . . And really, you know, he is as well as bedridden. It would be a marriage in name only. She would be more nurse than wife. She might be happy to exchange six months' work as a nurse, followed by a life as a respectable widow in fairly easy circumstances, for the future she now has, eking out a living as a teacher. She'd be a good mother for Roberta. If Grayshott married her, he would make her the child's guardian, one must suppose. Roberta would live with *her* and not Clancy. It might be worth putting it to her in that light, Max. It would save a long and costly court battle for Roberta. There is no saying we'd ever with the case either. Clancy is a ramshackle old fellow, but he wouldn't *beat* the child, or anything of that sort. It is only that she would grow up unmannered, in an extremely second-rate household, and marry some scoundrel . . ."

"Would she be better off with the schoolteacher in that respect? That woman might be anyone, for all we know. She is hand in glove with Miss Frisk and *that* set. A *third*-rate household, if ever there was one."

"Good gracious, I didn't mean Bobbie would go to live with her at Miss Frisk's place. They'd both stay at Andrew's cottage, right under our noses, and *we* would see to the hiring of help for the teacher and so on. In any case, from what I hear, the Sommers girl is from a good family. A connection of Strothingham on the mother's side."

"She cannot be connected to Strothingham or she would not be living as she does, in rented rooms, and teaching school. She's invented the story to try to nab herself a genteel husband."

"I don't know about that. She was in no hurry to nab Andrew, was she? The connection cannot be close, I suppose, but she is at least a gentlewoman. Miss Frisk tells me she attended a seminary, and can speak French and play the pianoforte — has all the accomplishments of a lady."

"Miss Frisk, of course, would be an excellent judge of such matters!" deVigne said with a sardonic curl of his lips.

"She knows the girl is above herself, at least. You cannot deny the influence would be *morally* good. One never sees Miss Sommers anywhere except at church and the lending library."

Driven to despair, deVigne allowed, with great reluctance, "It might be worth a try. But are we able to get Andrew sobered up and made presentable to go calling on her? For that matter, is he out of his bed at all these days? I haven't seen him outside the cottage for weeks."

"Lord, I hadn't thought of Andrew going in *person* to court her. His looks would be enough to disgust her, to see him run completely to seed."

"She's bound to see him if she agrees to marry him."

"*You* go and put it to her. Explain the situation. He is ill, dying in fact. Fill my glass, will you, Max? I come to rival Andrew in my drinking, but at my age it can hardly matter. Delicious sherry." She sipped carefully, then settled back to continue the discussion. "Miss Sommers will tend to his deathbed, then be Roberta's stepmother, living at the Cottage. Much better than wearing herself to a thread at the school. We would have to make some settlement on her as an added bribe — a few thousand pounds would be enough."

"I've never even *met* the girl. How could I put such a proposition to her? She looks a perfect little nun, mincing up the aisle on Sunday in those black gowns and plain round bonnets. *You* would be the more proper person to approach her, Jane. The nature of the arrangements would come more easily from a woman — the fact that it would be a marriage in name only, and so on."

"Use your head, Max! Your position as lord of the village must exert some influence. People are accustomed to doing as *you* wish."

"Miss Sommers is not. I've never had a thing to do with her."

"Still, your reputation — the very fact of your calling in person — would speak for the plan. You could use a little charm too, you know. It wouldn't kill you to *smile* at her, for instance."

"What, lead her to believe I have an eye on her myself? Nothing would be more likely to horrify a prude."

"Why do you say so? You ain't quite such an antidote as that."

"If she feels there is a position as my mistress as well as Andrew's wife in the bargain, she will view the scheme askance, I think."

"Oh, it won't be the position of mistress that pops into her head. You have very little notion of how a young lady's mind works. Just because she wears dark gowns and plain bonnets don't mean she isn't a romantic. All those trips to the lending library — it is always the *romances* she takes out. I know because she generally beats me to a new one. I wonder if she has returned *Evelina* yet. I am eager to read it. Why, I daresay she's been dreaming of nabbing you for years."

"Widgeon!" deVigne replied, dismayed at the charge.

"Ah, you've never been a girl, there's the problem. They always pick out the richest, handsomest gentleman within their view and dream about him. The more impossible it is they'll ever land him, the harder they dream. Smile, and tell her you would consider it a great personal favor, and you'll bring her around your thumb. See if you don't."

"Rather a shabby trick to play on the schoolteacher, don't you think?"

"Who are we interested in, the schoolteacher or Roberta? Besides, when she sees what a grouch and dictator you are, she won't be long in giving up on you."

"Thank you, love. I wondered how long your praise of my charms would go on before turning to its more customary abuse. Do you really think this plan has any chance of succeeding? I would happily play the fool for half an hour to secure Roberta's future."

"What have you got to lose?"

"Half an hour," he replied, and finished off his drink. "What time does the school close? I'll catch her there before she leaves."

"At three-thirty in the autumn, when the days are short. Wear your new blue jacket and drive the crested carriage. Give her the full treatment, and remember to *smile*."

"No, I don't plan to lead her on, but I'll outline the advantages to herself, and if she is sensible, as one hears she is, she may at least consider the offer. And then, of course, I shall have the delightful task of approaching Grayshott and seeing if he still favors the girl. I haven't heard him rant on about the soulful eyes for a year or so."

"I'll do that much for you. I'll do it now, before you go to the school, and before he has time to get drunk." She arose and was helped into her violet cape. "I'll stop back here on my way to the Dower House," she advised him, then was off through the park to tackle Grayshott.

The summer home built for Louise and Grayshott at the time of their marriage was a pleasant half-timbered cottage, hewn out of a corner of the deVigne holdings. It had deteriorated badly since Louise's death. The garden was overgrown; what had once been a lawn was now a pasture. The place needed paint, and the windows were dirty. Like its master, the place had been allowed to run to seed. Lady Jane's nose revolted at the dust and dirt within, but despite the unpleasantness of the surroundings in which the meeting took place, it was a success. Grayshott continued insanely infatuated with Miss Sommers. As he stumbled about the house in an alcoholic stupor, he thought often of her and Louise, who had blended into one ideal woman in his disordered brain. They were rather alike in their general appearance, both dark, handsome women. It was this which had first attracted him to her. He was not alert enough to realize he was past reclaiming, and still harbored the hope that he would win Miss Sommers. He assured Lady Jane in a weak voice that he would adopt a life of sobriety if the girl would have him. Yes, yes, he would be delighted to make her Roberta's guardian, in the unlikely event anything should happen to himself before his daughter was full grown. This he considered a very unlikely contingency. He never liked Clancy above half, and was only making him Bobbie's guardian to spite that stiff-rumped deVigne.

She darted back to the Hall. "Success! It is done. He still wants the girl. Mercy, but I doubt she'll have him if she gets a look at him. Hair flying down to his shoulders like a madman. You must get a firm promise from her, Max, or she'll bolt at the first glimpse of him. But he cannot last long. He's skin and bones. Go at once, and be sure you drop by and let me know what she said, hear?"

CHAPTER
THREE

DeVigne had no alternative but to press on with his half of the bargain. At three o'clock he had his crested carriage harnessed up, two liveried footmen standing behind to lend him consequence, his new blue superfine jacket on his shoulders, and a wary expression on his face. His timing was perfect. Out of the door of the schoolhouse erupted a stream of screaming students just as he drew up. Every one of them had to come and admire his carriage and horses before dashing off home to tell the parents deVigne was at the school. It was Mr Umpton who first saw him and ran out to make him welcome, but within three minutes he was in Miss Sommers's room, sitting atop a student's desk with his curled beaver in his hands and feeling more foolish than he had ever felt in his life, to put his preposterous scheme to this dignified gray-eyed woman who was looking at him in astonishment, and not friendly astonishment either. She appeared hostile, and he scarcely knew where to begin.

"How do you like teaching here?" he asked, to play for time.

"Fine. I like it very much," she answered calmly, wondering why he had come, and fearing Umpton had at last arranged to be rid of her. She had had words with Umpton only recently about her seeing some of his students after school. Lord deVigne was going to fire her!

"That's nice," he said, though it was not what he had hoped to hear. If she liked it, she would not be eager to leave, "Still, it must be a difficult life for a young lady." He didn't hesitate, even mentally, over the word lady. He had been pleasantly surprised to see that Miss Sommers was just that. Well-spoken, dignified, even pretty, with an elegance unrelated to her toilette but inherent in her bearing.

"The hours are long and work demanding, but I enjoy it. Why is it you have come to see me?" she asked immediately, when he had planned to broach the matter by degrees. Her eyes took in every detail of his splendor. A coat that seemed poured on his back, so well did it fit. An immaculate and intricate tie, above which his well-shaped head sat at a proud angle. Dark eyes, an aquiline nose, a lean face, with a touch of arrogance that was caused more by the arrangement of features than by his expression. Through the window she saw the impressive carriage, the footmen, and wondered at all this display, only to fire her.

"It is a family matter," he told her, after clearing his throat. "My brother-in-law, Mr Grayshott . . ." He noticed her face took on a wary look at the name. "You are acquainted with him, I believe?" His dark brows rose in a question.

24

She realized this was not mere chitchat. The visit had to do with Mr Grayshott. "I know him very slightly," she allowed.

"I beg your pardon?"

"I have met him twice, very briefly."

"But I understood — I thought you were better acquainted than that!"

"No, I was only speaking to him twice in my life."

"I see." He came to a standstill. The eyebrows settled down, and he blinked twice in surprise. She hardly knew Andrew, and here he thought there had been some romance between them. His proposition was clearly ineligible. A fool's errand. "I understood there was more to your relationship than that. I thought he had offered for you."

"He did. Twice."

DeVigne stared hard at her, out of penetrating, dark eyes. "He *met* you twice, and twice offered marriage to you? To a virtual stranger, in fact?"

"Yes, it was very strange," she agreed. "The first time ever I met him, he asked me to marry him. He was — he had been drinking, I believe, which would account for it."

"Very likely," he murmured, rapidly considering what to say next.

"What about Mr Grayshott? Has your coming something to do with him?" she pressed on.

He was favorably impressed with her and, though he was pretty sure she would not accept the plan, he decided to put it forward, having come this far. Indeed, he could think of no other way of extricating himself from the classroom. "He is not well, you know," he said.

"I haven't seen him about the village for some months now."

"No, he is ill. Very ill."

"I am sorry to hear it."

"Dying, in fact."

"Ah, that is too bad. It will leave his daughter an orphan." That's why he is come, she thought, her spirits lifting. I am at last to be offered the post of her governess, and I shall accept this time, if Grayshott is indeed dying.

"Yes, the reason I am come has to do with his daughter, Roberta." She smiled a little in anticipation. "She will be left under the guardianship of her uncle, Clancy Grayshott, when her father dies. It is not what we wish for her."

"Would you not be a more proper guardian, milord, being also an uncle?"

"I think I would, but there is some — disagreement between Grayshott and myself. We have not got along for years, since his wife's death. A family matter. So Roberta will leave the area and go to Clancy Grayshott, which the family is anxious to prevent."

"In what way can I be of help? I don't see what all this has to do with *me*."

As she was always rushing him on to the facts, he decided to blurt it out, and have it over with. "You could marry Andrew Grayshott. He still wants to marry you. If you did so, you, as her stepmother, would be appointed guardian. You would not be left alone in

26

charge of her. I — the family — would give you every help. We would be most eager to help you in every way. You would live at the Cottage — you know, I expect, where Grayshott lives?"

"Yes. Oh, yes, a charming place. But I must tell you before you say any more, milord, that I am not at all in favor of this plan. Twice I have refused Mr Grayshott in person, and I am not at all interested in marrying him."

"He is very ill, dying."

"Yes, but he's not dead yet, and who is to say he won't recuperate?" she asked frankly.

The possibility of this could not be totally ignored. He was rapidly drinking himself to his grave, but if he did actually engage in the life of sobriety he had mentioned to Jane, he might pull through. "I cannot guarantee his death," deVigne admitted.

"I didn't mean that! Indeed, I hope he does not die at all, but I cannot marry him."

"He likes you very much. Loves you, he says." This was a mistake. She drew back involuntarily, and he diluted the claim of passion as much as he could. "He is impressionable. When he cares for someone, he is eager to please her. He made my sister Louise a good husband; his drinking did not set in till after her death. If you married him, he might very well settle down and make you a good husband."

"No, he would not be a good husband for *me*. I dislike him intensely."

"Only think of the advantages. You would be freed from this life you lead. You say you enjoy the work, but you must confess it is hard on you, working every day from dawn till dark, with very little pay, and living in straitened circumstances. As Grayshott's wife you would live a life of ease, in a fine home that you could soon set to rights. You would be a respected member of society, with a carriage of your own, good company to visit, a completely different life from what you have now."

She brushed all this aside immediately and firmly. "The perquisites of the position are clear to me, clearer than they could possibly be to you who are not really aware of the alternative, but I do not wish to marry Mr Grayshott. My present life is not *that* distasteful to me. If it were a job you were offering, your niece's governess I had thought, then I would happily accept. I cannot enter into marriage with a man I actively dislike, do not respect at all. My past dealings with him were of a sort to make me very decided in this matter."

"The marriage would be only a formality, in his condition. The doctor feels he —"

"Yes, we have been through that, but still, he might live for years, and I do not wish to marry him."

"We had planned to make a settlement on you."

Her back stiffened at this. "Thank you very much, milord, but I am not for sale," she said, and arose from her seat to accompany Lord deVigne to the door. Perforce, he too arose and walked reluctantly behind her. It irked him to be the receiver of the last word instead of the giver. He was not accustomed to being balked, but in this affair he had not much hoped for success. He could have accepted failure if it had been more kindly worded, or more meekly.

"If you change your mind . . ." he said at the doorway, but she immediately overrode this suggestion.

"My decision is final," she said, with a certain set to her square chin that informed him to retire, before further angering her.

"Good day, ma'am. I am happy to have made your acquaintance," he said, and bowed and left to enter his carriage and return home, while the teacher stood at the door, smiling ironically at all his entourage, the footmen hauled out on this foolish errand. She must think him a coxcomb of the first water.

Delsie had been tired when he arrived, after her day; his short visit exhausted her utterly. She hardly had the strength to crawl home. If she had accepted, she supposed he would have offered to drive her. She climbed the stairs to Miss Frisk's attic apartment and threw herself on the bed. This is a new twist, she thought, sending his relatives to propose for him. What next, a minister with a ring, a choir hired, and a white veil? She shook her head and smiled, but in annoyance at their presumption, to think they could *buy* a person.

It was the first time she had spoken to Lord deVigne. He was not as she had expected. But, really, she had never satisfied him to look before. She made a habit of looking another way when he rode past, to show her uninterest. She found she had missed a good many interesting details. His hair, for instance; she had not noticed that it was worn brushed forward. The Brutus do, it was called. And the outfit — with a little gold watch fob shaped like a wishbone. Who would have thought deVigne was superstitious? His eyes, too, were darker than she had thought, almost navy blue. He had a commanding aspect which suggested to her he was not Grayshott's tool in the affair. Had the idea possibly originated this time from the baron himself? Was he that aware, then, of her existence, as to have known it was herself Grayshott would accept as a wife in this peculiar circumstance? And he never so much as glanced at her, or pretended to know she was alive, when they met in the street. To think that she, Delsie Sommers, was a subject of conversation at the Hall! It amused her to think of it. She accepted, after half an hour's musing, that there had been no trickery in it. DeVigne had come in good faith for the reason stated. It was plausible, if peculiar. And she had it in her power to thwart the wishes of Baron deVigne. She must be the only person in the village who had ever said no to him. This too amused, delighted her, to have the upper hand over those who rode past in their fine carriages with two footmen, ignoring her.

She hugged to herself the conquest. Those on the hill whom she had so long secretly envied now wanted her, and she would' not go to them. It was impossible not to consider how her life would have changed if she had agreed to marry Grayshott. No more teaching recalcitrant, ill-behaved youngsters, who wore one to a bone with their uninterest in learning. No more toadying to Mr Umpton, no more rising at seven. But better than that, to live on the fabulous hill, to walk up the aisle to church on Sunday with that august party. To drive into Questnow with them, and be bowed to in the shops, to be on the *inside* of all that life, it was hard to say no. She almost regretted her decision, till the image of Mr Grayshott darted into her head — drunken, dissolute, old, and with eyes that devoured her. She was quite sure he was mad. No, she had made the right decision, but it was the hardest one she had ever made.

DeVigne had his carriage and men sent on to the Hall and stopped at the Dower House to see Jane. The dame was waiting for him, peering through the lancet windows of her drawing room. "Well, what did she say?" she asked, before he had off his hat.

"No. She would not hear of it. Wouldn't consider it at all. She was paralyzed with shock, and so was I. Do you realize she only *met* Andrew two times in her life?" he asked.

"I knew he had not been courting her in the regular way. You didn't smile, or butter her up, I suppose?"

"She is not the butterable sort. Too stiff for that stunt. She has developed a schoolteacher's eye that made me feel ten years old and very gauche. She certainly knows her own mind, and doesn't hesitate to speak it, either."

"One cannot but wonder what set Andrew off on this passion for her."

"She's mighty attractive at close range," he went on, as they entered the drawing room and took up a seat. "The eyes, you recall, did the trick. Very fine eyes too, but hardly soulful. They were sparkling with anger throughout my visit. Andrew always had good taste in ladies. Louise was considered a bit of a beauty in her youth as well."

"What's to do, then? We must have Andrew committed and see a solicitor about getting Roberta without delay."

"Pity. She would have made such a good guardian for Bobbie. Very ladylike, and a firm hand on her."

"Too firm a hand is not what the child is used to. I wouldn't like that."

"I don't think she'd be *too* firm. There was some softer quality in her when she smiled."

Jane regarded him closely. "*She* had the wits to throw her cap at you, I see."

"Not in the least. It wasn't that sort of a smile. She thought we wanted a governess, and would have leapt at it. She'd be happy enough to get out of that school, I think. We'll wait a little, Jane, and see what develops, shall we?"

"What will develop is that Andrew will very soon die."

Over the next three weeks, Miss Sommers debated on and off with herself whether she had done right. Every morning at seven when she arose, with the day hardly bright, and put on her kettle to boil, she regretted that she was not between the linens at the mansion on the hill, having her breakfast in bed, but not for several hours yet. Cocoa she would have, not tea. As she walked briskly along the road, she would think, If I had accepted the offer, I would be in a carriage, not walking. And when she received her twenty-five pounds on quarter day, she thought: He mentioned a settlement. I wonder how much it would have been.

But these were only vagrant thoughts. On the whole, she knew she had made the wise choice.

Mr Umpton took a keen interest in deVigne's visit to the school. The true reason for his coming could not be told, so Delsie invented a different story to appease him, one having to do with becoming governess to Roberta at some future date. He didn't believe a word of it, and developed such a strong suspicion of her that life at school was nearly intolerable. Maybe he thought she was angling for his job. If a single student laughed or spoke loudly, he was at the door complaining of the noise. He complained too that the students coming to him from her class were ill-trained, couldn't read a word, and could hardly add two and two. He even spoke badly of her to his students, an unpardonable offense, so that they looked at her in a jeering way. The few who used to come after class for work no longer showed up. He spoke more than once of the mistake of hiring a woman for a man's job. "Next time we'll know better," he'd say meaningfully, implying that the next time was not far off.

The autumn wore on, the weather becoming colder, the days shortening, the winds growing more bitter, and the memory of the visit faded. She thought regretfully, once or twice a day, how fine it would have been if it had been a governess they were looking for, instead of a wife.

CHAPTER
FOUR

On the last Sunday in November, Delsie set her unadorned round bonnet on her head, looking in the mirror to see that it was straight. Her serious gray eyes looked back at her wistfully. She would have liked a prettier bonnet, at least on Sunday, but the schoolteacher was one who must dress discreetly. Dark clothing, she had been told. No curls, no powder, no scent, no jewelry of an ostentatious sort, Mr Umpton had announced, with a disapproving eye at her simple gold locket. I might as well be a grandmother, she thought, then wrinkled her nose at her reflection and went downstairs to call for Miss Frisk, who would accompany her to church.

Since they had arrived early, their heads, like everyone else's, turned when the party from the Hall entered. No company today, Delsie noted. Only Lord deVigne, Lady Jane, Sir Harold, and the young girl, Roberta, who came with them only infrequently. They entered their family pew, across the aisle and a few seats ahead of Miss Frisk and herself. The service progressed as usual, the hymns, and then it was time for the announcements. The vicar cleared his throat and looked around before speaking.

"I would like to ask the benefit of the prayers of the congregation this morning for Mr Andrew Grayshott of this parish, well known to us all . . ."

My God, he's dead! Delsie thought, and her eyes flew to the deVigne pew. So soon! Less than a month since Lord deVigne had asked her to marry him. I would have only had to live with him for a month: Surely it would have been worth it. I would be with them now, for the rest of my life. All this went through her head in a second. Then the minister's voice went on, ". . . who is very ill. Also for the repose of the soul of . . ." Lord deVigne's black head turned around over his shoulder. He directed a meaningful look across the aisle and back to Delsie, who was still staring at him, a question on her face. Their eyes met and, though no word was spoken, she was dead certain she would see him again that day.

After church, she went straight home and to her room. No "little chat" with Miss Frisk today. Within minutes — he hadn't even taken the others back up the hill, but had come to her directly from the church — there was a knock at her door. She had scarcely taken off her hat and hung up her pelisse. She assumed it would be Miss Frisk, big with the news that Lord deVigne awaited her belowstairs, but she was wrong. It was deVigne himself standing there, hat in hand, filling the small door frame with his size. "May I come in?" he asked.

"I'm not allowed gentlemen callers in my rooms," she told him. "We can go downstairs."

"I have spoken to Miss Frisk," he replied and, bending his head, stepped in.

"Oh — in that case . . ." It was unnecessary to extend any invitation. He was already inside, glancing around her apartment.

Never had her little rooms looked so bleak as they did today, as she imagined how they must appear to one accustomed to elegance. The shabby, threadbare rug, where dim outlines of flowers were all that remained of a once lively pattern, her homemade curtains and cushions, their unfaded yellow and blue stripes only strengthening the age of the rest, the worn settee to which she must lead him — all spoke of poverty and meager living. A vase of wilting flowers, weeds really, sat forlornly on the sofa table, and if he glanced through to her kitchen, he would see the breakfast dishes unwashed on the counter, for on Sundays she slept in and cleaned up after church.

"Pray be seated, milord," she invited, in the lofty tones of a duchess.

He sat on the settee, while she took up the one chair beside it. "You know why I am here?" he began at once.

"I heard the announcement in church. Mr Grayshott is ill — worse, I presume."

"Dying. He has caught pneumonia. There is no hope of a recovery. I have come to repeat my request of a few weeks ago. Will you marry him now?"

She shook her head. "It wouldn't be right. I can't marry a dying man."

"Your excuse — reason — on the last occasion I spoke to you on the matter was that I could not guarantee his death. I can now guarantee it, absolutely."

"I didn't say that!"

36

"It was your meaning. You said you couldn't marry him because he might recuperate. He is now beyond hope of it. All the advantages I outlined to you at that time still exist. You would be removed from this — place," he said, with a flutter of shapely hands, substituting a milder term than the word "hovel," which had first occurred to him. "You would no longer be required to work so hard for your living. For a few days spent as Mr Grayshott's wife, you would achieve independence."

"It's not right. Marriage is a sacrament. You should love the person. I can't marry for those reasons you give — for self-advancement."

"Marriage is also a legal contract. Think of it in that context. You would agree to take on the care of Roberta in exchange for a home and some security. It is a better position than the one you now hold."

"You don't understand," she said, shaking her head in confusion, for, while she felt bound to object, there had sprung up, back in the church, a strong regret that she had first refused. "How would it look to the villagers? I marry him one day, and two days later he is dead."

"You will have no trouble with the villagers. When you are seen to be under my family's protection, on intimate terms with us, they will not bother you. There will be a little unavoidable gossip, of course, but these things blow over quickly."

"On intimate terms with us." It was the most forceful argument he could have used. Her whole being longed to accept, but conscience held out. It wasn't right. It couldn't be right to do such a monstrous thing as marry Mr Grayshott. She tried, in a disjointed way, to put these thoughts into words. He nodded, but impatiently, frowning.

"Yes, yes, I understand your scruples. It is not the marriage any young lady would dream of, certainly, but still, it would be no bad thing for you. You needn't consider it as *selling* yourself, as you mentioned previously, the other time I spoke to you. It would be a job — you would have charge of Roberta, you would be working still, in a way. She needs a mother. That poor child has been badly neglected. She needs the care of a conscientious woman like yourself, someone to take a real and lasting interest in her welfare. She is scarcely ever allowed to come to us. She was with us today only because her father is so ill. It would be an act of charity on your part, certainly not taking advantage of anyone. No one loses anything by your accepting. Even Clancy Grayshott will be happy enough to have the girl off his hands. He only takes her to keep her from me. He will not be sorry to see her placed with an objective third party like yourself. Roberta gains a mother, you a good position in life, and you will be saving *me* a long and costly court battle." He spoke quickly, urgently, and convincingly, but still she was not quite talked over.

"I must have a little time to think, to consider it. I am sure there is something wrong with it. It doesn't seem right."

"Time is what we do not have. Andrew is dying. While we sit here talking, he might be drawing his last breath." He leaned forward from the settee, looking with those commanding eyes at her, pinning her to her chair, and his voice increased in pace, in urgency. "Think of yourself! Such a chance as this is not likely to come to you again, Miss Sommers. You live alone, and lonely I should think, in this crabbed little room. What company can there possibly be for a woman like you in this village? Whom do you see nights? The fishermen and their wives? What do you do for entertainment, relaxation? You are an educated, cultured lady, one prepared for better than this menial existence you lead. Your short life is being squandered away in this place. Come to us, to your own sort of people, and lead a normal life. There are times when we must act with promptness and decision. This is one of those times for you, Miss Sommers. Come with me now, or I think you will regret it all the rest of your life."

How had he known so accurately the points of her life to mention? She knew she would regret refusing. She swallowed and looked at him, uncertain, wavering.

"Come, there isn't a moment to spare," he said urgently, as he arose.

"Well, I'll come, then," she said, and she too got up, in a sort of trance, carried along by his words, his authoritative voice, by his very presence — the lord of the village. I still don't have to marry him, she thought to herself. I can think about it while we drive to Grayshott's house. If I change my mind, they can't *make* me marry him.

"Get your things together," he said.

"Oh — it will take a while. Can you come back later?"

"I'll wait. Where are your bags?"

She had only one, stored under her bed. She went into the bedroom and whisked her garments from closet and bureau in five minutes. Made a quick trip into the tiny parlor to pick up a few oddments, books, really nothing to show for her life's work, and was ready to go in ten minutes.

"I'll take your case." He picked up her bag, a large, square straw case, as easily as though it were empty, and very strange it looked, to see Lord deVigne carrying such a shabby article.

"I'd better say good-bye to Miss Frisk," she said.

"There will be plenty of time for that later. You can come back and call on her. Do you owe her any money?"

"No, I have paid for the month in advance." Just paid for December as well, but perhaps I'll be back, she added to herself.

At the door, he beckoned towards his carriage. A footboy sprinted forward and took her case. "See Miss Sommers to the carriage. I'll be with you directly," he added to Delsie, then stepped back inside the house. In less than two minutes, he joined her in the carriage.

"I explained to Miss Frisk," he said briefly.

"Explained in two minutes!" she objected.

"It would have taken a lady ten, which is why I chose to do it myself. I told her you would be calling on her soon."

"You take a great deal on yourself, milord!" That he had commandeered her life was atrocious, but it was this straw of his arrogance that broke her temper. *He*

40

would explain to Miss Frisk. *He* would decide that she would call soon.

"Forgive me," he said, with no trace of penance. "These are exceptional circumstances. You will not always find me so overbearing."

He placed a fur rug over her knees, and the horses bolted forward. It was an exhilarating experience, being *inside* a carriage, for once. To see others staring in at her, their eyes widening as they recognized her. She could almost read their lips. "It's Miss Sommers, the schoolteacher!"

"We'll go directly to the Cottage," he told her. "That's what we call Mr Grayshott's place. The wedding will have to take place immediately, while he's still conscious."

"No — not so soon! I wanted time to consider it."

"You have had a month in which to consider it, ma'am. Did you not regret your former decision? Tell me truthfully now, as you plodded to school in the early morning, or lay in your bed at night, did you not feel you had been overly hasty? Under this new circumstance of Andrew's imminent death, are you not agreeable to marry him?"

Was the man a mind reader? She looked at him, much struck at his percipience. But when she spoke, she uttered an irrelevance. "How did the rest of the family get home? Surely you didn't leave them at Questnow?"

"No, Sir Harold brought his coach today as well. I knew mine would be required to bring you and your effects to us."

"You *knew* that, did you?" she asked ironically.

"Hoped," he modified, with no more shame when it was needed than humility at his former arrogance.

"I suppose you arranged as well for the vicar to be there, *knowing* he would be required?"

"Certainly I did. The marriage could not be performed without him. He went with Sir Harold. The solicitor also will be there, to see to the will."

"Well, you have forgotten one rather important detail, milord. There have been no banns read, and we cannot be married without a license in that case!" she stated triumphantly.

"You are surely not under twenty-one?" he asked.

"I am twenty-two, but still a license is required, if I am not mistaken."

"Only twenty-two? What a strong character you have, for one so young."

"About the license . . ."

"I have a license, Miss Sommers. I took the precaution of procuring one two days ago, when Andrew first came down with pneumonia, in case it should be necessary in a hurry."

"I daresay you have got a gold band in your pocket as well," she said, resigned to his omniscience.

"Did you want a gold band in particular, ma'am? I have selected a rather pretty circlet of diamond baguettes. I hope I chose the right size."

She hadn't a doubt in the world he had. "My bridesmaid and best man?" she inquired, suppressing a fierce urge to giggle.

"Lady Jane and myself. You have no objection?"

42

"None in the least. Where are we to go for our honeymoon?"

"No honeymoon will be possible, I'm afraid," he replied blandly. "But you are young yet. There is no saying you will not have a *real* marriage before too many years, if you are interested in it at all."

"I will be sure to put *you* in charge of arranging all the details," she said, then stopped short, as she realized what freedom she was taking with the almighty Lord deVigne.

"You couldn't do better," he answered readily. Offense, like humility and shame, was missing when she expected to see it. He spoke on calmly, as though they were out for a Sunday drive, no more. "There will be a good many bothersome details in this business. As I have coerced you into the match, I shall attend to them all, to give you as little worry as possible."

"That is very kind of you, but I have been accustomed for many years to looking after myself, milord."

"The experience has left its trace on you. I do not mean that as a criticism. Quite the contrary."

"I would appreciate being consulted at least on any details that have a direct bearing on me."

"I will bear it in mind, ma'am," he agreed, nodding at her.

"I must notify Mr Umpton I will not be at school tomorrow."

"Or any other tomorrows."

What a pleasing phrase! A wave of complete exultation washed over her, to be at last free of Umpton and the students. He spoke on, apparently unaware of her feelings. "I understand Mr Umpton's cousin, a Mr Perkins, is interested in the position. Shall I get in touch with Umpton?"

After her protest at independence, it was too cowardly to ask him to do it, yet it was the one chore she would happily have relegated to him.

"You will be busy, and in some state of perturbation as well in all the excitement. Let me do it for you," he suggested, in a rather final tone that indicated the matter was settled.

"Thank you, if you would be so kind," she said meekly.

Before it seemed possible, the carriage had climbed the hill, with the metallic table of glittering sea stretching below them, an incredible view really, but little appreciated today. They pulled up outside the half-timbered cottage where Mr Grayshott lay ill. DeVigne looked at the unkempt yard and building, then glanced at his companion. "All this mess can be cleared away very easily," he assured her.

Sir Harold's coach was already there, and a gig belonging to the solicitor. It seemed less possible every moment for Delsie to retreat from her decision, to refuse to marry him. The so-much-wanted time for reconsidering did not exist. DeVigne ushered her into the house, where an unpleasant odor assailed her nostrils, but before she had time to look about her, she was being hurried upstairs, with a stream of chatter to divert her, to prevent her thinking about what lay ahead. They walked along an uncarpeted hallway, knocked at a closed door, and were bade to enter. Mr Grayshott lay propped up on pillows in a handsome four-poster bed, with his valet bending over him. He had been prepared for the ceremony, with his tails of hair trimmed, his face shaven, and a dressing gown of peacock hues over his thin shoulders. Still, to his bride he looked like a caricature of his former self, with his face shrunken almost beyond recognition and turned to an alarming graying tone. Clearly there would be no recovering from such an advanced state of decline.

He held out a hand and said in a weak voice, "Come in, Miss Sommers." She entered, reluctantly, and deVigne came beside her. "Leave us, Max. You too, Samson," Grayshott said to his valet. Delsie cast one wild, imploring look to deVigne. His fingers tightened reassuringly on her arm before he left, with Samson departing from another door. She stood alone with her bridegroom.

"Come closer," he said. She advanced to the side of the bed. He reached out a hand to her, and in confusion, she put hers into it. "Miss Sommers — now I may call you Delsie — at last it is to be." He referred, she presumed, to their marriage. "You have made me wait too long," he said sadly. "Still, you are mine at last, and we shall have a few months together at least." Her heart fluttered at this grim forecast, but of course it was nonsense. He was at death's door. Perhaps they had led him to believe it, to get his agreement to the marriage.

She half feared he might close his eyes and expire even while she stood with her hand in his. He sighed, but a stronger pressure from his fingers told her death was not yet at hand. "There is so much I would say," he began, with his eyes closing. "You will be kind to my little Bobbie. I know that much. Promise me you will take care of her."

"Yes, I promise."

Again he squeezed her fingers, while she looked at the wizened face before her. "You will not regret it," he went on, weakly. "The cottage and her mother's portion are for my daughter. It was arranged by deVigne, but the rest of it is yours — payment for this favor you do me. There is money, you know. I have money." He got his eyes open, with some effort, and looked at her closely.

"I do not do this for money," she said. Grayshott's fortune, she knew from deVigne, was dissipated.

"For love?" he asked, and smiled ironically. She said nothing. This was carrying hypocrisy too far. She could not say she loved him. He lifted the hand he held to his lips and kissed it, while she stood rigid with embarrassment and shame, and even anger. Then he fell into a fit of coughing. "Better get on with it," he said when he had recovered. "Call deVigne."

She was heartily glad to leave the room in search of him, and hadn't far to go. He stood outside the door, a few feet down the corridor, with the vicar, Lady Jane, and Sir Harold, and no doubt the solicitor too was not far behind, though she didn't actually see him. The whole party entered Grayshott's room, except Sir Harold, who went below. The bride stood beside the prostrate bridegroom, and the vicar, opening his book, began to intone the solemn words of the marriage

46

ceremony. How inappropriate they sounded — "to love, honor, and cherish . . . to have and to hold . . . till death us do part . . ." It was a moot point whether the groom would last out the ceremony. Grayshott held her hand tightly throughout the reading, repeating those portions of the service that ritual decreed. "I, Andrew Grayshott, take thee, Delsie Sommers . . ."

Best not to think. Think about something else. In five minutes it will be over — I can leave. Miss Frisk is having her lunch now. No school tomorrow, or any tomorrows. DeVigne is not wearing his good-luck charm today. I wish I were wearing it. I think I'm going to giggle — I think I'm going crazy. Where shall I go when this wedding is over? Do I remain here, in this house? No doubt deVigne has arranged all details. She repeated her words, parrotlike, and soon the circlet of diamond baguettes was being pushed on to her finger by Andrew. It had the weight of a pair of manacles, and though it was pretty, she felt a strong urge to pull it off and throw it out the window. Then they were signing papers, people were shaking her hand — so foolish — the vicar wishing her happy. My God, what must he make of this travesty? What subtle pressures had deVigne brought to bear, to make him go through with it?

"Leave us now," Grayshott said to them all. "I want to be alone with my bride." Delsie cast a frightened glance to the little group, then looked to her groom. "Don't worry, Max, you can send in the solicitor in five minutes. Leave me five minutes' privacy with my wife," Grayshott said, his voice fading.

They left, but the ceremony had tired Grayshott, and the five minutes were not so harrowing as she had feared. She sat beside him, while he held her hand, his eyes closed, his lips smiling. He looked frighteningly like a death mask. "Talk to me," he ordered.

What did one say to a man at death's door, a man, besides, whom one had just married without caring for him in the least? She decided to talk of his daughter. "I shall take good care of Roberta," she began. "I shall try to be a mother to her. I am used to dealing with children. I am — was — a schoolteacher, you recall." He nodded, satisfied apparently with this line, and she rambled on, making much of nothing.

After an interval that was surely at least five minutes, he opened his eyes and said, "You'll do. There is money — I should tell you where. It's not easy. I'll tell you later, when I feel stouter. I saved it for you, for . . ." Then he fell into a coughing fit again, and it was clear he was nearly spent. There was a tap at the door. DeVigne entered, with the solicitor at his heels.

"May I go now?" Delsie whispered to him.

He nodded. From the bed a weak voice followed her. "Come back after, Delsie. I'll tell you where . . ."

"Your wife will return to you after luncheon, Andrew," deVigne said. "She has had a busy morning. She will want her luncheon."

"After lunch," he nodded, and Delsie escaped out the door, down the stairs to the main saloon, where Lady Jane and Sir Harold sat talking to the vicar. They all looked toward her. "Lord deVigne and the solicitor are with him," she said, and sat down, too overcome to take part in any conversation.

The vicar turned to her. "This has been a very romantic affair," he said, smiling. "A long-standing attachment — a pity you waited so long, Miss Sommers."

She looked at him, bewildered. Before she had said anything, Lady Jane came forward and pushed a glass of wine into her hands. "Drink this, you'll feel better," she said.

Sir Harold engaged the vicar in some ecclesiastical talk, and Lady Jane turned to Delsie. "We had to give vicar some story. He thinks you and Andrew have been in love for some time."

Delsie nodded and sipped her wine. She was relieved that the vicar at least was acting decently in the matter.

In a short space of time, deVigne and the solicitor descended. The doctor arrived and went abovestairs to his patient, while the solicitor offered the vicar a ride back to Questnow. As soon as the family were alone, Delsie said, "Must I come back after lunch?" Her face, though she didn't know it, was ash-white, her eyes two large dark circles.

"Just for a moment," deVigne said. "I doubt he will even be conscious. It is nearly over, Mrs Grayshott."

"Oh!" she gasped. It was the first time she had been called by her new name. She found it singularly unpleasant.

"Let's get out of here," Lady Jane suggested. "Enough to give anyone the blue devils, looking at this dust-laden room."

They all arose, with no argument. DeVigne took Delsie's arm and led her to his carriage, and the others followed in Sir Harold's, the two making a brisk trot to the Hall. Seeing the Hall at such close range, actually entering its twin portals, would have been a matter of great interest on any other occasion. Today, Delsie entered in such a state of distraction, she spared not a glance at the surroundings. She was vaguely aware of approaching a large stone home, with leaded windows gleaming in the pale autumnal sunshine, and the vines just turning to autumn colors along the windows' edges. She was similarly insensible to aged oaken woodwork within, the curving great staircase with intricately carved ornaments on posts and ceilings. The size and furnishings of the large saloon into which she was shown were also ignored. She walked to the fireplace and stood looking into the leaping flames, with her hands stretched out to them. Her hands were cold as ice.

Her three companions exchanged a look, wondering what to do about her. DeVigne poured a healthy portion of brandy, Jane added a dash of water to it, and handed it to her. "Try this," she said.

Delsie sipped obediently and choked, being unaccustomed to the strong drink. But in small sips she finished the glass, and felt a little restored. It took the cold chill from her bones as the fire had not done. It was more an emotional numbness than a physical chill.

"We'd better get on with luncheon if we are to go back to the cottage," deVigne suggested.

"Must she go, Max?" Lady Jane asked, with a condoling look at the bride. "She doesn't look up to it."

"I promised him," Delsie said. "I'll go." Then she set down her empty glass, lifted her chin, and accepted deVigne's arm to enter the dining room.

CHAPTER
FIVE

With such a small company, just the four of them, luncheon was served in the breakfast room, where no effort had been made to treat the occasion as a wedding feast. The silverware and china were finer than Miss Sommers was used to. A large bowl of late roses, in shades of pink, decorated the center of the table. There was an abundance of meats she could not relish in her state, but with gratitude she accepted a glass of wine. One glass a day was more than she usually took; this morning she had had three drinks in fairly quick succession. Her head began spinning, and she changed to water. That was her luncheon — a glass of wine and a glass of water. The others scarcely ate more.

"Well, it is done!" Lady Jane said, with a note of satisfaction.

"Leave it to Max," Sir Harold added by way of a compliment, and lifted his glass.

They then abandoned the subject, and began to speak of other things. What did Max think of Sir Harold's paper on Goethe? Hearing only one word in ten, Delsie was struck with the odd fact that Sir Harold had no small talk — he discussed only philosophy and weighty matters of eternal interest, while his wife was just the opposite. She rattled away about the flowers or a gown or a servant, but hadn't a word to say on her husband's conversation. What an odd pair, she smiled inwardly — but not so odd as Mr Grayshott and myself.

After luncheon, she was again led to deVigne's carriage, and the short drive down the hill to the Cottage was executed. She sat silent, thinking her own wandering thoughts, while her finger played with the wedding ring. It fit perfectly. As they turned in at the gateway he said, "This is the worst of it. It will soon be over with," in a bracing way.

It was over sooner than either of them thought. They were met inside the door by the doctor, who told them Mr Grayshott had passed quietly away in his sleep half an hour before. It was as though a great weight slipped from her back. She felt light; giddy with relief. Perhaps she had been harboring the dread that he might recover, that she would actually have to live with that shell of a man.

"I'll take Mrs Grayshott home, then," deVigne said. He too sounded relieved.

"This is my home now," she pointed out, with a downcast look at the Cottage.

"There will be no need to spend the night here. It is not fit to live in yet. Lady Jane had your bag taken to her place. You and Roberta will spend the night there, and come here tomorrow or the next day. You won't want to be alone tonight."

She didn't want particularly to be with a stranger either. "Couldn't I go back to the village?" she asked.

"This business is already irregular enough that we shouldn't add unnecessarily to it," he pointed out, kindly but firmly. "You are leaving that life behind you. Don't look back."

The advice, she supposed, was good. She had often enough wished she were out of it. Back into the carriage, which already seemed to be second nature to her. There was no feeling of grandeur attaching to it now, but only a welcome haven from the brisk winds of November. They went at once to Lady Jane.

The Dower House was a stone building like the Hall. It was three stories high, done in a Gothic style, lancet windows, pointed roof, and even miniature flying buttresses, ornamental very likely, as it was not huge enough to actually require that support. There was a fine wrought-iron fence around the place, shoulder high, through which it was necessary to pass by foot as the gates were rusted shut at an angle too narrow to allow the carriage to pass. This seemed to be the only feature of the house that was not in first repair, however. All was neatly trimmed, windows shining, a pleasant change from the cottage. DeVigne left his carriage standing at the gate and took her to the door, indicating that he did not mean to enter. He left her in the hallway with Lady Jane. Sir Harold was in his study, reading some Latin manuscript he had on loan from the Bodleian Library.

"Come into the saloon," Lady Jane said kindly, examining her new relative minutely for lingering signs of shock.

54

Delsie was sufficiently recovered to appreciate this room. Cozy — there was not that feeling of being in a cathedral she had experienced at the Hall, but perhaps that had been due to her emotional state. It was done in gold tones — velvet settees, the wooden pieces large and substantial, from an older period. A bowl of chrysanthemums was nicely arranged with ferns on a mahogany table. Delsie's gaze settled on this.

"What does one say at such a time?" Lady Jane asked frankly, then laughed. Looking into those dancing blue eyes, Delsie had a smile coaxed out of her. "Not condolences, I shouldn't think," the dame rattled on. "It must be a great relief to you he passed on so quickly. Good riddance say I, and may the Lord forgive me if it's wrong."

Mrs Grayshott was relieved there was to be no charade of her being a grieving widow. "What a dreadful thing to say, but I am not the least sorry," she admitted.

"No more you should be! There's no point in our whispering and wearing long faces, as though you were a real widow, is there, my dear? Of course not. Such nonsense. Let us just sit down by the fire and have a nice coze, and become acquainted, as we are connections now. It's nice to have a new family member to chat with, and a female too. I have missed the luxury. You must be happy to be out of the parish school. A *killing* job for a lady."

"Yes, like the death of Mr Grayshott, I cannot pretend to any sorrow over it. It was horrid."

"Leave it for the men. They get all the good things in life, let them take the bad along with it. I'll call for a cup of tea," Lady Jane said, nodding in approval of her own sensible sentiments. "I noticed you didn't take a bite of lunch. Pity, the asparagus looked very good. I'll have Max send some over for our dinner. He has excellent succession houses. We never want for fresh fruit — oranges and pineapples. So, Miss Sommers — oh, dear! *That* will never do — Mrs Grayshott. I daresay you like that even less. May I call you Delsie? That is your name, I believe?"

"That will do very well, milady."

"Well then, Delsie, we have a few things to discuss. Though *entre nous* we are not to pretend to any sort of mourning, the proprieties must be observed in public. Do you have mourning clothes?"

"Yes, I have my things from my mother's death. I shall need a few more gowns now that I am — here." She hardly knew what words to use to indicate her awareness of the superior surroundings in which she now found herself.

"A few gowns for evening wear, I think. We dress for dinner, though I shouldn't think you and Bobbie will bother when you dine at the Cottage together. But we don't mean to abandon you there in the least. We are all one big happy family here. Usually Max dines with us, or we with him. I should be quite talking to myself otherwise, for my husband is not at all sociable, nor can we leave Max rolling around all alone in that big castle, you must know. It would be too cruel. Andrew took no part in our get-togethers, but we hope you mean to do so."

This pleasant method of taking meals and probably passing an evening sounded delightful, and, with a thought to her narrow wardrobe, Delsie realized she would indeed require additions to it. "I should be happy to join you," she said.

"After you have got the Cottage set to rights — a shambles, is it not? — you shall take your turn of entertaining us as well. Now, about other matters than mourning clothes, there will be callers coming for the next few days. They ought not to do so till after the burial, by rights, but every person one knows *will* do it, thinking he is the only one, and that company will help. So what we must decide is where to greet them. Or do you want to meet them at all? Max feels the proper time to reveal the wedding — I should have said announce, but with such a hole-in-the-wall affair, reveal sounds the proper term — anyway, Max thinks it should be done at once. Let the village get over the shock of it as soon as possible, and while there is the death to help take their minds off it. It will be less uncomfortable for you to meet people as Andrew's widow at the funeral calls, when they must maintain a decent decorum. Can't be asking too many prying questions of a widow, and if they get too far out of line, you can always draw out a handkerchief and start dabbing at your eyes. Max and I will give a good snub to the first one who tries it. Are you any good at a snub yourself, Delsie?"

This drew forth a light laugh. "I snub students very well, but I confess I haven't much experience of snubbing anyone else."

"Ah — that surprises me. I took the notion from Max that you might have given him a good set-down when first he went to you."

"Not intentionally. How do you go about it, milady?" she asked, quite at her ease. She would never have foreseen getting along so well with Lady Jane, who had looked the toploftiest of deVigne's relatives, next to himself.

"Max has it down to an art. Raises those black brows of his, pinches in his nostrils, and says 'Indeed?' in a certain tone. He has the face to pull it off, that one. Lacking his elegance, I look the culprit dead in the eye and think of a rat. I loathe rats. Then I say 'Really?' — drawing it out a little, or 'Do you think so?' or something of the sort, depending on what has preceded. But I shan't have too much setting-down to do. I have come up with a plan, you see. You saw the first step of it this morning, with the vicar. It is not entirely unknown in the village that Andrew has had this passion to marry you the past two or three years, for the gudgeon told everyone he spoke to about you. Frankly, my dear Delsie, there has been more than one nosy Parker asking why you didn't take him. So I mean to imply that the marriage had been planned some time ago for the Christmas holidays, which will explain your not having given any notice yet at the school, and then it was rushed forward when Andrew took ill. All a faradiddle of course, but I have only to imply to Mrs

Gardiner and a few of my cronies that you hadn't planned to marry quite so soon, and it will be set about in no time. I daresay vicar has already told half a dozen. Not even a lie, really, for you had no idea of ever marrying him at all, till Max made you do it."

"That sounds feasible," Delsie admitted, with an admiring look at her astute friend.

"I enjoy scheming and conniving," the lady admitted. "It helps to get in the days. There will be the suspecting few who think you only did it to insinuate yourself into a soft position when you knew Andrew was dying, but they won't dare to say so. Not to *you* at any rate, and we need not care what is said over the teacups in Questnow."

What a wonderful way of life! Not to care what was said over the teacups in the village. For the village teacher, what was uttered there was of vital importance. The wrong utterance could spell the end of the job.

"The next thing to decide is the where of it," Lady Jane went on. "On such an occasion, I expect it is to the Hall that people will go first, to offer their sympathy to Max. Might be best if we are all there *en masse*. The Cottage cannot be got ready in time, so it is there, the Hall, or here."

"What will Lord deVigne expect?" she asked. She could not accuse herself of opting out of this decision. Surely it was for the family, the real family, to decide this matter, and not a stranger like herself.

"He always prefers the Hall for everything," was the unhesitating answer. "Max has a paternal streak a mile wide. He would like to think he is *my* father, considers himself very much Bobbie's, and will be trying to lead you as well if you give him half a chance. On this occasion, however, it would be as well to let everyone see the marriage has his approval, not to say connivance."

"It was all his doing," Delsie said at once. "I didn't even know I meant for sure to go through with it, till I got there and saw the parson waiting."

"I'm sure you hadn't a word to say about it. I nearly fell over when I saw he had even got a ring, and it isn't Louise's either. He would have the sense not to buy it in the village. He found time to dart over to another town to pick it up. He is thorough, you must allow. Once Max has made up his mind to a thing, it is as well as done. It was not *all* his doing, however. *I* thought of it, and Max only carried it through. He is open to suggestion. I'll say that much for him. He is *reasonably* domineering. His papa, who was my cousin Pierre, was *unreasonably* domineering. He married my sister."

"Is there French blood in the family, ma'am? The 'deVigne' would lead one to believe so, and you mentioned Pierre."

"Some Norman ancestors a couple of hundred years back, I believe. We never speak of it. My cousin Pierre, I was telling you, was an utter tyrant. He made Max look like a puppet. Take some crackerbrained notion and stick to it buckle and thong. But you are not in a mood for family anecdotes today. We'll get to that another time. We must learn all about each other. What I began to say, but I always get diverted, is that Max

60

can be steered, if it is done cleverly and openly. Be open with him, it is the best way."

"It is my own way of dealing, Lady Jane."

"Good. Now, have you any questions? A million of them, I daresay, all rolled up in a ball. They'll fall loose one by one, and you must just ask me as they occur to you."

"I am too confused to be methodical. One thing that *does* interest me very much is Mr Grayshott's daughter. I understand she is here with you. I should like to meet her. What sort of a girl is she?"

"Ah, Bobbie, our little baby!" she exclaimed, with a softened expression and a glowing eye that told her listener that whatever else the girl was, she was the apple of this lady's eye. "She's six years old and has been motherless for more than three of those years. Louise died in childbirth, an unhappy event that has had very bad effects on the whole family. You may expect Bobbie to be different," she finished, inadequately. "She has had a succession of nursemaids and lately a governess, a Miss Milne, whom I procured for Andrew. A good sort of a girl. Bobbie is bright — not a great beauty, worse luck. She has a strong look of her father about the eyes, and his unfortunate coloring. Brownish hair, but Louise's pleasant smile and disposition. Her manners are not what they should be, but I am sure you will take care of that. You'll meet her later today. Max sent her home from church today with Mrs Beecham, a friend of mine. He knew there would be confusion, with the wedding and all. He'll pick her up and break the news to her. It won't be so appalling for her as you might think. She was not close to her father. Well, you know the way he's been lately. It will be better for you both to stay here a few days till she gets used to you. Rather hard on her to be set up with a total stranger at this time."

"I hadn't thought of that. Too wrapped up in my own problems. It will be difficult for her. I hope we will get on together."

"You will. It will be good for her to be able to get used to someone — someone who will be with her for more than a few months. The girls minding her lately never stopped long, what with Andrew's behavior. She is at loose ends. I tried to mother her as much as I could, but when I wanted to have her here, Andrew invariably took the idea that I was Max's accomplice trying to get her moved to the Hall, from whence she would nevermore return to him; so I only saw her there at the Cottage, and it was not as good as one could wish. However, I hope you will let me have her for a day now and then, and yourself too. How cozy we shall be — three women — 'girls' of all ages — to sit and gossip and giggle together. I am a great gossip; I love it, and I daresay you can tell me all the doings of the village. Is it true the butcher beats his wife?"

They enjoyed a long and entertaining gossip before Lady Jane suggested it was time to change for dinner. Max was coming, and she must haul Harold away from his tomes and see that he put on a clean shirt.

Sir Harold, Lord deVigne, Lady Jane, and Delsie were soon seated round an oval table in a large dining room, where the death and subsequent arrangements made up the dinner conversation, which was not so lugubrious as might be imagined. It led Sir Harold to an exposition on Milton's "Lycidas," an ode mourning the death of a friend, interspersed with more down-to-earth matters by his spouse and deVigne. It was hammered out by the three not interested in Milton that deVigne would be in charge of the funeral arrangements, and the callers would be greeted at the Hall.

"No formal announcement of the wedding will be made at all, with your approval, ma'am," deVigne said to Delsie. "It is so singularly inappropriate to do so at this time. We shall say in the death announcement that he is survived by his wife, Mrs Grayshott (née Delsie Sommers) and his daughter, Roberta. That will be announcement enough. There is no question of its being overlooked. You will be presented as Mrs Grayshott to the callers, and, as Jane so cleverly pointed out, a funeral call is no time to be overly curious as to the details."

"Delsie is staying here with Bobbie for a few days, Max," Jane told him. "Let the child become accustomed to her new mama while there is at least one familiar face around, in case she makes strange at first."

"An excellent idea," he agreed. "It will be a difficult period for Bobbie. It will give us time to send a few servants to the Cottage to clean it up a little as well."

"A lot," Jane countered. "It will require a small army."

"Is there anyone of your family you wish to notify of your marriage?" Max asked next.

"No, there is no one," she answered quietly.

"Strothingham ought to be informed," Sir Harold mentioned.

As Sir Harold was so seldom aware even of important facts, his wife was astonished to learn he had come into contact with a rumor. Her eyes flew first to Sir Harold, then to deVigne, lastly to Delsie, who wondered that the lady should look embarrassed.

"I am not personally acquainted with my cousin, Strothingham," Delsie answered. "Indeed, I have never so much as seen him."

"Still, head of your family. Ought to be informed," Sir Harold told her. "I'll do it myself, Mrs Grayshott. Not a close friend of Strothingham, but I was a crony of his uncle's. Once told him I'd look you up, in fact. Did I ever do it?" he asked with a puzzled frown.

"No, I don't believe you did," she answered, staring at him, as people were inclined to do when first becoming a little aware of his peculiarities.

"Bless my soul! What a memory I have. Shocking," he said calmly, and went on eating, while Lady Jane, and deVigne threw up their eyes in despair.

"Then the only remaining piece of business is to introduce you to Roberta," deVigne said. "I brought her back with me. She is abovestairs with Miss Milne now. We shall speak of the running of the Cottage another time, Mrs Grayshott."

Her jaws clenched at the use of that name, Mrs Grayshott, but her mind harked back to Sir Harold's curious speech. He had known Strothingham, had

64

known all this time she was related to him, had even promised to look her up. How different things might have been, had he done it.

After dinner, Lady Jane said she would bring Roberta down, but Delsie asked if she might go up to her instead. She wished the first meeting with the girl to be informal, in private, that she would not feel constrained to be stiff because of the onlookers. Her experience of children told her this was the better way to start off the friendship.

"A good idea," Max agreed. "As I have already spoken to her of you, I shall make the introduction, if you have no objection?" He was overly careful, she thought, of consulting her on these matters since she had given him the hint.

"None in the world," she replied, and they went together to the room Roberta was using as hers during the stay at the Dower House. She was a very ordinary-looking child. Mousy brown hair in pigtails, eyes distressingly like her father's, but she had a winning smile, the absence of front teeth emphasizing the childish, vulnerable air.

"This is the lady I told you about, Bobbie," he said. "Your new mother, Mrs Grayshott."

Delsie watched with amusement and a pang of sympathy as the child clung to deVigne's fingers, jiggling back and forth shyly, while casting little peeps at herself.

"We're going to be good friends," Delsie said encouragingly, and put out her hand.

A little set of pink fingers reached out to take it. "Are you a wicked stepmother?" the girl asked, not in a condemning way at all, but in a spirit of curiosity.

"I hope not indeed!"

"I believe I may have inadvertently used the term stepmother," deVigne explained.

"The 'wicked,' I trust, was her own invention?"

"*All* stepmothers are wicked," Bobbie told her conclusively. "They step on you. I hope you're not a *hard* stepper."

"I shall try not to be as wicked as most," Delsie assured her, then led her to the edge of the bed to sit down, to remove the obstacle of height. "I never beat little girls, or starve them, or hardly ever lock them in a dungeon, if they behave well."

"Max has a dungeon," she was told. "He'll never lock me in it."

"You must show it to me one day. I've never seen a dungeon," Delsie answered.

"I will. It's got big thick doors and no windows. It's black as coal."

"It sounds lovely."

"It is. I wouldn't care if you locked me up in it forever. And you can't turn my papa against me, because he's dead," Bobbie added, knowing the role of stepmothers very well.

"I think I may safely leave you two adversaries to discover each other's evil propensities," Max said with a smile, and left. He returned below to announce that the two were in a fair way to becoming acquainted.

"She will know how to handle the child," Jane informed him with satisfaction.

As Roberta did not dwell on the subject of her father's death, Delsie was happy to avoid it, and spoke bracingly of future projects they would undertake together. She was promised a view of not only a dungeon, but a walking doll and a dog who had fleas. While the last-named did not sound very exciting, she was eager to see the dungeon and the walking doll. When the governess came to prepare Bobbie for bed, Delsie told her that for this one occasion she would like to perform this task, to prolong the meeting. She saw that the child was in sore need of mothering, for her garments, outside of her dress, were small for her, and in poor repair. The two got on well together, the older sensing in her new charge that same unsettled quality she had experienced herself, and an eagerness to attach herself to someone.

It was close to an hour before she returned downstairs to find deVigne just leaving. "I shall spend the night at the Cottage," he told her.

"The Cottage? What in the world for?" Lady Jane inquired. "The Bristcombes are there."

"They are old-fashioned," Max replied. "Mrs Bristcombe, I noticed, was putting a dish of salt on the coffin to keep the corpse from rising, and as she follows the old customs, she will likely light a candle to propitiate Satan as well. We do not want Mrs Grayshott's house to be burned to the ground before ever she moves in."

These old folkways were well known to Delsie, but for herself, she would not much have cared if the house did burn down. She did not in the least look forward to removing to it.

After deVigne had left, Sir Harold asked her for a game of chess. This sounded preferable to further lessons on Milton, and she was happy to oblige him, for it always fagged her brain to the point where sleep came easily.

CHAPTER
SIX

The next few days passed with a mixture of joy, embarrassment, and serene contentment. They were never boring. The meetings with the funeral callers were a strain. There was no denying that fact; even with the family at her back she felt foolish to be presented as the bride of a dead man nearly old enough to be her father, one, besides, whom she scarcely knew. But as wise old Lady Jane had predicted, prying questions were kept to a minimum. Delsie smiled to herself to see deVigne poker up, pinch in his nostrils and say "Indeed?" when a neighbor from the far side of the hill began a discussion on her shock at reading of the affair in the papers. She knew Jane was also busy visualizing dead rats, for she would hear all about it after the company had left. Few questions were directed to herself, and those that were, she fielded easily enough, for she wore a downcast, bewildered face, and the quizzing was not severe.

The periods with Bobbie were joyful. Such a blessed relief to have the throng of children to which she was accustomed, mostly rowdy boys too, reduced to one fairly well behaved girl, who already looked to her as a surrogate mother, and was beginning to run to her with her secrets and problems. Time was found for a few walks in the afternoon with her stepdaughter, to further the acquaintance. When the callers were done with, the family would gather back at the Dower House to sit and gossip and even — it seemed incredible — to laugh occasionally. This, in her private thoughts, Delsie considered the happy hour. With the day's duties done, she could relax. She had quickly come to the stage where she was perfectly at ease with Lady Jane, and no longer on tenterhooks with deVigne, though they still addressed each other formally, with always that "Mrs Grayshott" irking her. Then there was dinner, a formal meal, whose elegancies she was able to appreciate now as she had not on that first, dreadful day of her wedding.

She had been married on Sunday. The funeral was Thursday. On Friday the idyll was over. DeVigne came over after breakfast to take her to the Cottage, her new home. "I'll tell Miss Milne to prepare Bobbie's things," she said, and excused herself.

"I'm sorry to see them go," Lady Jane said to her nephew. "It was good to have a spot of company. Harold is as dumb as a dog, unless I let him talk my ear off about Rome or Greece. It was a wise move, Max, to push this marriage."

"It seems to be working out very well for *us*. I can't imagine Mrs Grayshott will be as happy at the Cottage as she has been here with you."

"How happy can she have been in Questnow? What a strange, lonely life the girl has led. Little things she says betray her, you know, like how pleasant it is to have company for her meals. She must have eaten all alone, I suppose, since her mama's passing. Imagine that ninny of a Harold having known Strothingham all along and not telling us. We might have made her acquaintance years ago."

"She was living in a very mean sort of an apartment. Remarkable she is so refined."

"I was happily surprised with her liveliness. I had not suspected vivacity from her, for she was such a dowdy little dresser, but she is very conservable. I like her excessively."

The widow soon returned below with Bobbie and Miss Milne, the three of them to be taken in deVigne's carriage to the Cottage. Once there, he did no more than make her acquainted with her housekeeper before leaving, saying he would return later in the day.

"You will find plenty to keep you busy," he said, glancing around at the somber surroundings. "But I shan't volunteer any suggestions, knowing you like to make your own decisions." This was said in a rallying tone, but it did not rally her. She felt utterly depressed, and the large beef-faced woman standing before her in a soiled apron did nothing to cheer her up.

"I'll take my leave now, Mrs Grayshott," deVigne bowed, and went to the door. Delsie looked helplessly to the governess and Bobbie, fast disappearing up the stairs, then after deVigne. She took a step after him, wishing she could run right out the door and go back to the Dower House. As she realized what she had done, she continued after him, as though, it had been her intention to accompany him to the front door.

"Don't despair," he said in a kindly tone. "This was used to be a fine and attractive home a few years ago, when my sister was alive. You will make it so again in a very short time, I am convinced. Be firm with the Bristcombes. They have fallen into slovenly habits with Andrew not watching them as he ought." Mrs Bristcombe stood with her arms crossed, staring at them suspiciously, beyond earshot. Then deVigne was gone, and Delsie turned back to face her future.

Be firm, he had said, and firmness was clearly needed here. "Have you any orders, miss?" Mrs Bristcombe asked, an insolent expression settling on her coarse features as soon as deVigne was gone.

"Yes, the title is *ma'am*, not *miss*," Delsie said in her firmest teacher's voice, "and I shall have a great many orders. The first is that you put on a clean apron, and not wear a soiled one in my house again."

"They don't stay clean long in the kitchen," the woman replied tartly, scanning her new mistress from head to toe in a very bold fashion. She had not behaved so when deVigne was with them.

"Then you must have several, to provide yourself a change, must you not?"

"Muslin costs money."

"All of three shillings a yard, for that quality. I shall buy some, and you will have it made into aprons."

Mrs Bristcombe's steely eyes narrowed, but she pulled in her horns. "What'll you have for lunch?" she asked.

"What have you got in the house?"

72

"There's cold mutton, and a long bill overdue at the grocer's, while we're on the subject."

"Why has it not been paid?"

"The master's been sick, as you might have *heard*," she replied with a heavy sarcasm, to reveal her opinion of the marriage.

"Prepare your accounts and present them to me in the study this afternoon, if you please. The mutton will do for luncheon, with an omelette. You know how to prepare an omelette?" Delsie asked, to retaliate for the former insult.

The woman sniffed, and Mrs Grayshott continued asserting her authority. "I am going to make a tour of the house. There is no need for you to accompany me. Miss Roberta will come with me."

"You won't find it in very good shape."

"So I assumed," Delsie replied, looking around her. "I understood girls were sent down from the Hall to tidy the place up."

"They've changed the linen upstairs and cleaned up the yellow guest room for you."

"Thank you, but I am not a *guest* in this house, Mrs Bristcombe. I shall notify you what chamber I wish cleaned for me. Good day." She turned and swept up the stairs, resolved not to let that Tartar get the upper hand of her, though she was weak from nervousness after the encounter.

She walked along the upstairs hall till she heard voices. Bobbie and Miss Milne were putting off their pelisses, and she requested Bobbie to show her around the house. "I'll show you *my* room first," Bobbie said proudly. "This is it."

"I thought you would still be in the nursery," Delsie answered. The room was not unpleasant, but it was not a child's room. The furnishings were of dark oak, the window hangings and canopy of a somber, dusky blue. The paintings on the walls were also dark and not likely to appeal to a child.

"I wondered when I came that she was not in the nursery," Miss Milne mentioned, "but I was told this is her room."

"Mrs Bristcombe told you?" Mrs Grayshott inquired, in a voice a little taut.

"Yes, ma'am. I took my directions from her. I seldom spoke to Mr Grayshott."

"I had to leave the nursery last year, 'cause I couldn't sleep with all the noise," Bobbie told them. Delsie thought this referred to noises made by a drunken father, and asked no more questions, but the child spoke on. "Mrs Bristcombe said it was the pixies in the orchard," she said, her eyes big. "Daddy said it was the pixies too, so I got this nice room, like a grown-up."

"In the *orchard*?" Delsie asked, surprised that Mr Grayshott would be allowed out of the house drunk. One would have thought his valet or Bristcombe would have kept him in. She must ask Lady Jane about this.

"I have thought I heard noises outside myself, from time to time," Miss Milne said, rather hesitantly, as though she were unsure whether she should speak, "If you won't be needing me right away, ma'am, I'll go to my room and unpack."

74

"Go ahead." The girl left, with a rather shy smile. She would make a friend. It was a good feeling, to have one person of her own age and sex in the house, one not too far removed from her in breeding as well. The girl seemed polite and well behaved. Her chief interest, however, was in her new stepdaughter, and she turned to her with a determined smile. "How about showing me that walking doll you spoke of? I never heard of a doll who can walk. Do we have to hold her hands and pull her along?"

"Oh, no, she walks all by herself," Bobbie boasted. "Daddy made her for me. Well, he didn't 'zactly *make* her. He bought a plain doll, and Mommy cut her stomach open, and Daddy put in some little wheels, and now she can walk." As she spoke she went to a shelf where a considerable quantity of stuffed toys were set out, the only concession to the room's being inhabited by a child. "Daddy was very smart, before Mammy died. He made a secret drawer in Mommy's dresser that opens with a hidden button."

She selected a doll dressed in a sailor's uniform, reached under the jacket to wind a key, and, when the doll was set on the floor, it took half a dozen jerky steps before toppling over. "He doesn't walk too good," Bobbie said, setting it back up for another dozen steps.

"How ingenious! Your daddy *made* this?" Delsie asked, sure the child was inventing this story. But when she took the doll up, she saw that the stuffed body had indeed been slit open and sewed up.

"He made me a cat that shook her head too, but I broke her," Bobbie said, then took the doll to throw it on the bed. "Next I'll show you Mama's room. It's the nicest one. I think you should use it, only it's quite far away from mine."

They walked half the length of the hall, then Bobbie opened a door into a lady's chamber of considerable elegance, though the elegance had begun to fade. It was done in rose velvet, the window and bed hangings still in good repair, but very likely full of dust. The furniture was dainty French in design, white-painted, with gilt trim. There was a makeup table with lamps, an escritoire — such a room as Delsie had only dreamed of. The late Mrs Grayshott's belongings were still laid out — chased-silver brushes, cut-glass perfume bottles, and a whole battery of pots and trays holding creams, powders, and the accessories to a lady's toilette. "Let us see the yellow room Mrs Bristcombe made up for me," Delsie said, with a last, longing look at this room.

"It's this way, next to mine," Bobbie told her, and led her to a good room, square, but with none of the finery of the lady's chamber. Like Bobbie's, it faced the west side of the house, away from the orchard. "You won't be bothered by the pixies either," Bobbie told her. "Likely that's why she put you here. Miss Milne sleeps right next door."

They did not disturb Miss Milne, but went along to look into other chambers, the master bedroom (which opened through an adjoining door into the late Mrs Grayshott's suite) being the end of the tour.

"Since you're my mama now, *I* think you should sleep in here," Bobbie said firmly.

76

It was all the inducement Delsie needed to make the charming chamber her own, and she said, "I think so too, but then I shall be away from you and Miss Milne. Let us look again at the room next to your mama's."

"It's the primrose suite," Bobbie said, and entered again, enjoying very much playing the guide.

"This is one of my favorites," Delsie said involuntarily, looking at the springlike walls, sprigged with flowers. The curtains were done in apple green with white tassels, and the furniture light and graceful. "I wonder you were not moved into this room," Delsie mentioned.

"It's on the wrong side. The pixies," Bobbie answered.

"I have a feeling the pixies won't bother us any longer," she answered with a smile. "Stepmothers, you know, are very powerful creatures, and the pixies never bother us. Miss Milne could use the room next door to yours, and we three would all be close together for company." This seemed important to the widow, to be not too far removed from other life in the house.

"Let's move my stuff, then," Bobbie suggested at once.

"We'll speak to Miss Milne first, shall we?" This was done, with the practical suggestion coming from Miss Milne that the chambers be cleaned and aired first. When Miss Milne went for dustcloths and brooms, Delsie found herself at loose ends, and to get in the morning, she took to herself the task of doing up her own room. It was a pleasure to restore the lovely furnishings to their proper state of gloss, to clean the mirror and polish those cut-glass bottles, to arrange her few gowns in the clothes press. She would have the hangings taken down and the carpet raised for beating before the snow began to fly. The hours till luncheon flew past happily.

"Can I eat with you, Mama?" Bobbie asked when the job was done.

"I hope you don't plan to make me eat alone!" Delsie exclaimed. No other course had occurred to her. "Miss Milne, you will join us as well, I hope?"

Miss Milne seemed pleased at the invitation, and the three went down together to wash. When Bobbie twice addressed her new stepmother as Mama, Delsie smiled in contentment and said nothing. To put the matter on a settled basis, Bobbie herself brought up the point. "Since you're in Mama's room now, I must call you Mama." So she explained her action.

"Of course you must, my dear," Delsie replied matter-of-factly.

Mrs Bristcombe had not actually said she knew how to make an omelette, which perhaps accounted for the greasy mess served up at that meal. While taking the housekeeper to task on that account, the widow forgot to ask the woman to please make up her bed, but really, the poor woman did seem to be overworked. There did not appear to be another female servant in the house, except for the governess, who obviously could not be expected to do it. She would find clean linen and do it herself.

After luncheon, it was time to turn Bobbie over to Miss Milne for lessons, but before doing so, she discovered of them the location of the linen closet. It was a large walk-in cupboard, with several rows of shelves, nine tenths of them empty. When she took her own linen, there remained in the place exactly two towels, and no bed sheets. Must ask Mrs Bristcombe about this.

When the bed was finished, she went to the study to meet the housekeeper on the matter of the accounts, and they had an unpleasant conversation over unpaid bills of such staggering sums that Delsie was surprised the grocer had not set up a public clamor. When queried about the lack of linens, the woman said firmly there was not another bit or piece of material in the house. Nothing had been replaced since Mrs Grayshott's death, and the old ones were so full of holes, with no one to mend them, that she'd torn them up to use for rags.

"It seems very strange to me," Delsie said severely, not willing to relinquish a single point to her adversary. "I suppose I must get some new ones."

"If you think it's worth your while," Mrs Bristcombe answered mysteriously, then arose and left.

Delsie sat pondering that statement. It sounded strangely as though the woman didn't think she'd be staying long. When the front-door knocker sounded, she went herself to answer it. Unaccustomed to servants, she did not find this so strange as a lady from a well-ordered home would have done.

DeVigne was surprised to see her come to the door, and asked where Bristcombe was.

"Does Mr Bristcombe work here as well?" Delsie asked. "I haven't a notion where he may be. I have not had the pleasure of meeting any of the servants except Mrs Bristcombe, and I use the word 'pleasure' in its loosest sense, I assure you."

"She should have assembled them for your inspection and orders," he mentioned.

Delsie was intelligent enough to realize then that she should have had this done, but how was she to know? She had never had a single servant to command. "Shall we go into the study? I have had a fire laid there, where I have been going over accounts with Mrs Bristcombe. A harrowing pastime, I might add."

They entered the study and took up the two uncomfortable chairs nearest the grate. "Things are in a muddle, are they?" he inquired. "I can't say I'm surprised. Andrew was in no case to attend to business, and resented any interference. Have you managed to figure out the extent of his debt?"

"If I have all the bills. They were handed to me in a box, loose. No records of any sort kept. I make it roughly a hundred pounds!" she said, wide-eyed at such a sum. "That is a whole year's salary."

"A teacher's salary?" he asked, his lips unsteady.

"That is what *I* was paid at St Mary's, though I believe Mr Umpton made considerably more."

"Of course he would. He is a man," deVigne answered, unwisely.

"He was not hired as a *man*, but as a teacher, like myself. Of course a man must support a family," she added grudgingly. It had pestered her, this fact of

Umpton's making twice the salary she made, for doing half the work.

"You will be happy to hear you are better situated financially now," deVigne informed her. "I have been to the solicitor, and wish to discuss money matters with you. Louise's portion was twenty-five thousand pounds. The interest of that amounts to twelve-fifty yearly for the running of the Cottage. It is not a large sum, but —"

"Not large? It is a fortune!" Delsie contradicted bluntly. "Of course, the expenses on such an establishment as this must be considerable. Is there a mortgage on the house?"

"No, the family built the house as a summer cottage for Louise and Andrew as a wedding gift. It is Roberta's now, in trust till her maturity. The expenses certainly *are* considerable. There are the servants to be paid and kept. Louise's portion was never meant to carry the whole. Andrew was well fixed when they married, but he ran through his capital with gambling and mismanagement after his wife's death. You know the story. The Bristcombes have been receiving two hundred annually, along with their room and board, and the governess is paid seventy-five — less than a teacher," he pointed out with a mischievous smile. "When we are fortunate enough to have a governess, that is. The other servants —"

"Excuse me, milord, but I have been wondering about that, I don't see any other servants about. Mrs Bristcombe does everything — everything that gets done, that is to say. She does the cooking and ordering of household supplies, and it was she who laid the fire. There doesn't seem to be another soul in the house, except Miss Milne."

"This is absurd," deVigne said at once. "There is Betsy Rose, the downstairs maid, and I'm sure there was an upstairs maid as well. Naturally Andrew's valet, Samson, has left, but there was used to be a footboy to help Bristcombe, though I think he left some while ago. The Bristcombes cannot be doing the whole of the work themselves."

Delsie ran a finger along the top of a table, and it came away covered in dust. "I cannot believe there is a Betsy Rose here any longer," she said.

"We shall certainly have to see about that. I had thought the total costs for servants would amount to about four-fifty, which would leave you eight hundred to run the place. Do you think you can do it? There is food and fuel, but much of both come from the Hall. There will be general household costs and maintenance, along with stable expenses . . . No, it can't be done. You will do better to use my carriage, unless you wish to use your own money to set up a Tilbury or landau."

"My money?" she asked, startled, then looked away in embarrassment. Where had he taken the idea she had any money of her own? Surely he must have realized from her style of living that she had none. "I don't have any money," she said simply.

"You have five thousand pounds," he told her. "I explained when we discussed your marrying Andrew that a small settlement would be made on you. It is not much, but it is your own, to do with as you wish. You would be wise to leave the capital intact and use only the interest, but that, of course, is quite your own affair."

She was on her feet in revolt. "I cannot possibly take such a sum! It would be — *immoral!*" Oh, but wouldn't it be lovely? Fifty years' salary.

"It is business, Mrs Grayshott. We agreed to the settlement. It was inherent in our deal. In fact, it is done. I told you I had been to the solicitor. Your actual salary, if you use only the interest, will not be so much greater than your stipend at St Mary's, and your costs, I fear, will be higher. Well, a carriage for one thing, and you will want to buy some personal effects, very likely."

Casting an eye down at her black gown, which she was so heartily tired of seeing, she saw the justice of his words. "It seems a high price to pay, only to have a guardian for Bobbie."

"She is my niece, my only niece. There is no way I would prefer to spend the money."

"It still seems a great deal of money."

"If it makes you feel better, Sir Harold and myself share the cost. We were both happy to have the matter settled so quickly and so felicitously. The court costs to acquire guardianship of her would have been great, to say nothing of the inconvenience and unpleasantness of such a course. Nor is it at all certain we would have won. So, that matter is taken care of. Can you hold house on fifteen hundred a year? I include your own money in the figure."

"Certainly I can. I must be a wretched manager if I could not. There is a grocery bill I should like to settle at once. How do I arrange to pay the bills?"

"You may turn the matter over to me, or, if you prefer — as I suspect you do — I shall put the income from Bobbie's trust in your hands for you to draw on from the bank."

"That would be better."

With a smile, he handed her a bankbook. "You see, it is not *always* necessary for me to consult you on matters. I come to realize how you prefer to have things done."

She took the book and opened it. "Why, Mr Grayshott hasn't spent a penny of the income the whole year! The year nearly over too — December. What do you suppose he used for money all the while?"

"I have a sinking sensation we shall discover he has been living on tick. His credit would be good. I shall put a notice in the papers, with your approval."

"You have my approval," she said with resignation. "And you needn't feel it necessary to consult me on every little detail."

"How shall I know in what areas you consider me competent to exercise my own judgment?" he asked, in a tone which she suspected was not entirely serious.

"I referred only to personal matters. On those I should like to be consulted."

"Surely the handling of money is a highly personal affair."

"In this case, it is Roberta's money, for the most part, that we are discussing."

84

"You are now her legal guardian. The finances are entirely in your capable hands. They could not be in better ones, in my opinion, ma'am."

"Thank you. I *do* mean to be careful of her monies. And there is something other than money I should like to discuss with you. I would like to be rid of the Bristcombes."

"So soon?" he asked, startled.

"She is impertinent and slovenly and — and I don't like her," she finished, less sure of her ground.

"You are the mistress here. If you wish to be rid of her, then by all means turn her off."

"What do *you* think?" she asked, for she could see very plainly that he disliked the suggestion, for some reason.

"I think you judge on very little evidence, Mrs Grayshott. You have not been here above half a day. She does appear slovenly, and the house, of course, is in wretched shape, but if she is indeed doing the whole herself, it must be taken into consideration. The Bristcombes have been with Andrew for years, stood by him all through his illness. Dismissal seems a poor reward for such faithfulness. As to the impertinence, may I inquire what form it took?"

"She called me 'miss,' for one thing."

"A slip of the tongue, I should think. I have had the impression over the past few days that you dislike my calling you Mrs Grayshott. Is it not so?"

Again she flinched at the name. "I *do* dislike it, but it is my name now, and I must get used to it."

"It is inevitable you will be addressed so by outsiders, but within the family, I think we might spare you, as you dislike it. I notice the others have circumvented the use of it. Jane calls you by your given name, and Bobbie will certainly call you Mama ere long."

"She already does!" she interjected happily.

"I am so glad! I have seen with pleasure her growing admiration for you, and knew it must come to 'Mama' within the week. 'Mama' will hardly do for myself, however. Can we not hit on something less galling than Mrs Grayshott?"

"It will not do to call me Miss Sommers," she pointed out, with a rising curiosity as to what he had in mind. She had a strange notion he meant to call her 'Delsie,' and would not have objected to being asked to address him as 'Max' either.

"No, that was not the alternative I had in mind. Shall we make do with the catch-all word *cousin*? I call many of my connections who are not actually cousins by the term."

"I have no objection," she allowed, feeling unaccountably let down. To have thought a week ago deVigne would be calling her "cousin" would have been incredible.

"While we are about renaming ourselves, do you think you might dispense with the 'milord'? My name is Maxwell. The family call me Max, or just deVigne, without the 'Lord'."

She nodded, and decided on the spot that as he had not called her Delsie, he would remain deVigne till hell froze over.

86

"Another item settled, cousin, to our mutual satisfaction, or almost. Shall we drink to it? In this house above all others, I shouldn't think there would be any scarcity of wine."

She found a decanter on the sideboard in the dining room and brought it and two glasses into the study DeVigne's eyes grew at the size of the shot she poured out, but he said only, "Thank you," and took a careful sip, while Delsie took a longer one and promptly fell into a spasm of coughing.

"What is it?" she gasped, when she recovered her speech.

"It is brandy, and very fine stuff too. French. Smuggled, of course. Trust Andrew. It is to be sipped, by the way, not tossed off like lemonade. If I may make a suggestion."

She glared at this repetitious poking fun of her desire to have things in her own hands. She set the brandy aside. "We were speaking of firing Mrs Bristcombe," she said in a businesslike way. "You think I ought to wait and see if she improves?"

"I would do so. It sets people's backs up needlessly to fire servants. We are desirous just now of not drawing any unfavorable attention to ourselves. It is up to you, however."

She regretted very much her lack of experience in such matters. The woman seemed impossible to her, but perhaps all servants were bothersome. The gentry did seem to be forever complaining of their servants. "I'll wait a little," she decided, "but I suspect that as well as being slovenly and impertinent, she is also dishonest. How many sheets did your sister have when she married?"

He looked astonished at the question, and shrugged his shoulders. "I couldn't say. Perhaps two — three dozen. May I know why you ask?"

"There was exactly *one pair* in the linen cupboard, and where did they go? That is what I should like to know!" she said, nodding her head.

"It is close to a decade since Louise married. They are worn out, I suppose."

"She has only been dead three years. Two or three dozen sheets do not wear out so quickly. They have been stolen. And not more than a pair of clean towels. She must have had two or three dozen of them as well, and from the looks of the people in this house, I cannot believe that towels were worn to patches, whatever about sheets."

"You take your hoarding of Bobbie's monies and chattels very seriously, cousin. Replace what you need, and keep count of them. You'll soon learn if you are being bilked. Have you run into any other problems, besides vanishing linen and house-keepers who call you 'miss'?"

"Only the pixies, but I suppose you know about *them.*"

"No, I don't. Do tell me, what have the pixies been up to? Stealing the preserve jars?"

"No, they have been frightening Bobbie. Did Mr Grayshott roam about the grounds drunk at night?"

"Not to my knowledge. He drank to excess, of course, but I never heard anything about his roaming

88

outside the house in such a state. I cannot think Samson would have permitted anything so dangerous."

"Someone, Mrs Bristcombe in fact, told her the noises in the orchard at night were pixies, and so she had to sleep on the west side. I have moved her to the east, hoping the pixies have made their last racket. I am taking the late Mrs Grayshott's suite for myself," she added with a defensive look, ready for objections.

"I should think so. It used to be a charming suite. We had the furnishings imported from France. No doubt you will secrete your pin money in the secret compartment Andrew installed at the back of one of the drawers for Louise."

"Bobbie mentioned it. I have not seen it yet. He was quite ingenious with mechanical contrivances, was he not? Bobbie showed me her walking doll."

"It was a hobby with him. I have an extremely ugly clock at the Hall I must show you some time. He fixed up a mantel clock for me, the face of it inserted in the stomach of a blackamoor, engineered in such a way that the fellow's eyes move with every tick. It annoyed me so, I had it removed to a guest suite. It is one of Bobbie's favorite toys. When will you be bringing her to see me?"

"Does she go to you often?"

"Not till the present, but I hope to see you *both* there frequently, now that matters are more congenially arranged. I shall have the pleasure of your company this evening, I trust? We are to dine there. I'll send the carriage for you at six, if that —"

"Yes, it meets with my approval," she told him, with a baleful stare that concealed her joy.

"One would never guess it from that black scowl, cousin," he answered, and arose to leave.

CHAPTER
SEVEN

Dinner with the family, whether at the Hall or the Dower House, was always a civilized, happy interval in the day, looked forward to as if it were a party. She knew from comments made by Lady Jane that larger parties were held as well, but in this period of mourning, it was only family. Till she was more sure of her footing, Delsie was happy it was only family. She looked forward to holding her own first dinner party at the Cottage. On this evening, Lady Jane brought forward a subject of great interest to the widow, a shopping trip to the village on the morrow. Delsie had made a list of items required for the Cottage, herself, and, even more urgently, for Bobbie, whose wardrobe was in sad need of replenishing. She was happy she would make her debut in Questnow under the unexceptionable chaperonage of Lady Jane. She hardly feared any direct insults, but the villagers, used to thinking of her as one of themselves, might be jealous of her sudden rise to prominence.

After dinner, she discussed with Lady Jane what she meant to buy and where the best price might be found. DeVigne and Sir Harold had a game table drawn up to the other side of the grate and had a game of chess. At eleven o'clock, Lady Jane began yawning, and it was the signal for the company to take its leave. She and Harold walked to the Dower House through the garden that separated the two buildings. It was not a long enough distance to require having their carriage put to. DeVigne was to see Delsie home. With a pleasant glow still lingering from the evening, she was surprised when his first question after they were ensconced in the carriage was, "I expect you find the time at the Cottage lonesome, with only Bobbie for company?"

"Oh, no! I was very busy all day with my bookkeeping, you recall, and getting settled in."

"You will soon make new friends, to call on you and to visit in turn. It is the mourning that keeps our circle so close at this time."

She had not the least desire to see the cozy circle enlarged by so much as one. "I suppose so," she answered.

"For the present, you must feel free to visit Aunt Jane if you are lonesome, or bring Bobbie to me, as I mentioned. I am home a good deal in this weather."

"I won't be lonesome," she said, and smiled softly to herself. How wonderful to have whole days to herself, with no school. It was like a long, perpetual holiday. "Oh, but I didn't mean to be unsociable. I shall take Bobbie to Lady Jane, of course."

"Also to her Uncle Max, I hope. I mentioned *two* homes where you will always be welcome, cousin."

Twice he had mentioned it. She hardly knew what to say to so much condescension, and said, "Thank you."

"I did not mean to give the impression I was bestowing a favor. Quite the contrary. *I* am sometimes lonesome too."

It was a novel thought to ponder, that deVigne, with his mansion and his carriages and his arrogant face, should ever be lonesome, but perhaps he was. Still, she could not quite envision herself walking boldly to his front door and asking for him.

When they reached the Cottage, the house was in utter darkness, looking strangely ominous, with the untrimmed shrubbery reaching black arms into the path, and with the building itself a black hulk, lightened by the irregular paler shapes of the plaster in the half-timbering. She was reluctant to enter. "I should have told them to leave some lights burning," she said. More inexperience on her part.

"It should not have been necessary. Any sane servant should have known enough. You'll have a job on your hands reforming the Bristcombes, it seems. At least they have not locked you out. The door is on the latch."

They entered into a perfectly black hallway, where deVigne fumbled at the table to light a lamp. Of the Bristcombes not a sign was to be seen. "I wonder if he locked up before going to bed," Max said. A check of the side door in the study revealed it was locked, and they assumed the kitchen quarters to be safe as well. Delsie locked the front door after him and took the lamp up the stairs to light her way. Even with her lamp, she found it rather frightening to be going alone down the black hallway, in a strange house. She peeped into Bobbie's room, to see the child sleeping soundly, looking so innocent and vulnerable, with her little hands, open palms up, on the pillow. The child was her responsibility now, an awesome task, really. Strange how she was coming to love her, yet she had the very eyes of her father.

She went into her own room, lit another lamp, and prepared for bed. She took up a volume of poetry from Louise's bookshelf and brought the lamp to her bedside table to read. It was with a feeling of sheer luxury that she looked at her watch, read the hour as well after eleven, and knew it was not too late. There was no need to be up at seven. She would read till midnight. She was relaxed, happy, looking forward to the shopping trip tomorrow, when she extinguished her lamp at midnight and fell into that light doze that precedes sleep. Before she was quite unconscious, her arm was rudely jostled. She jumped in her bed, her heart pounding.

"They're back," a soft voice said, giggling at her alarm.

"Oh, it's you, Bobbie," Delsie said, shaking herself awake. "You frightened the life out of me. Who is back? What's the matter?" she asked, thinking in her confusion that the Bristcombes had been out, and that was why the house had been plunged into darkness when she returned.

"The pixies," Bobbie said.

"Poor dear, you've had a bad dream. There are no pixies tonight. Were you frightened? Come and get into bed with me if you like. There's plenty of room."

Bobbie took immediate advantage of this tempting suggestion, and popped in with her stepmother. They were both sleepy, and were about to nod off when a slight sound was heard from the window. "It's the pixies, Mama. I told you they were back," Bobbie said, yawning in mid-sentence, as she snuggled deeper into the bed, no longer afraid of the pixies when she had protection.

Mrs Grayshott listened, soon incontrovertibly aware that something was going forward in the orchard beyond her window. That it was either pixies or the ghost of her late husband never so much as occurred to her. It was only the ignorant, superstitious folks such as the Bristcombes who believed in pixies and putting a dish of salt by a corpse to prevent its rising. The sounds obviously came from a live, human trespasser, whose identity interested her. She slid quietly from her bed to avoid waking the child, who was already breathing deeply, asleep. Tiptoeing to the window, she pulled back the curtains and strained her eyes out into the darkness. Nothing was visible. There was no moon, and the phalanx of low, spreading apple trees successfully concealed whatever was causing the noise. For some minutes Delsie remained, looking and wondering. She quietly opened the casement window and stuck her head out. The noises were more easily audible now, though they were still low noises, as of stealthy movement. She could hear the rattle of a harness, or chain, and the soft clop of hooves, moving slowly forward. Some indistinguishable sounds of human voices too, male voices, she knew. Men were in the orchard, with a horse or horses. What could it mean? The only conclusion she could come to was that some poor neighbors were stealing apples. The crop surely had been harvested by such a late date, but the windfalls perhaps were being taken up by some poor family. With a shrug of her shoulders, she closed the window and climbed back into the warm bed, not unduly disturbed, but determined to check the next morning to see if she could discover trace of the intruders. Familiar with the pinch of poverty, she did not begrudge the taking of the apples, but she would prefer in future that permission be asked. Foolish of them to have waited so long, too — December. The apples must be inedible by now.

There was no sleeping in the next morning, with a wide-awake six-year-old in her bed, eager to be up and doing. The girl was up bright and early. Glancing at her watch, Delsie saw it was only seven. How quickly she had become accustomed to the luxury of sleeping in! But rest was impossible with the wriggling child hinting every minute that it was bright, so she dragged herself out of bed, and put on her frock while Bobbie skipped down the hall to dress herself. With a pang of sympathy for the lower orders, she told the girl not to awaken her governess. However, when Bobbie returned to her, her braids were neatly made up, and clearly it had not been her own childish fingers that had formed them so well.

They went downstairs, to find no breakfast awaiting them at such an hour. Mrs Bristcombe seemed startled to be run to earth in her kitchen, a single glimpse of which quite revolted Delsie for the filth all around.

Another battle to come over this before the day was done. The kettle was not even on the boil. Mrs Bristcombe was given orders to have breakfast ready by eight, and the ladies of the Cottage went outdoors for a walk. With a memory of the commotion in the orchard the night before, Delsie elected to walk there, though she would not disturb the child with an account of what had occurred.

To call it an orchard was really to overstate the case. There were only thirty trees, six rows of five. From the number of apples on the ground, and the state of them, it seemed highly unlikely it was this that had drawn the intruders. The apples were beyond eating, for the most part. They had been through several frosts, leaving them brown and withered. A few still clung to the branches, their skins puckered. This waste shocked the thrifty ex-teacher. It was too late to save them this autumn, but next year they would be gathered before they had turned. She observed that two trees growing in the midst of the others were dwarfed for some reason — noticeably runted compared to the rest. The apples did not appear to be of any different kind, so that could not account for it. She looked about her for signs of intruders. Clearly the men had not come for apples, so what had brought them? She could see no wheel tracks in the grass. There were considerable signs of traffic, the grass well trampled, with here and there in the earth the outline of what might have been horseshoes.

Bobbie was playing about, looking for edible apples on the ground. "Why are those two trees smaller than the others, do you know?" Delsie asked her.

"Those are the pixie trees," the child answered.

"What do you mean?"

"That's what Mrs Bristcombe calls them, the pixie trees. They are the best ones in the orchard too, even though the smallest. She says they are worth more than all the others put together."

Again Delsie looked at the apples still remaining on the dwarf trees, comparing them to those on the others. She picked one in better preservation than the others and tasted it. It was a plain pippin, tasty but not delicious. She walked to the other small tree and examined it. It too was just an ordinary tree, dwarfed for some reason. The soil perhaps was not good in these two spots, though it seemed odd, right in the middle of the small orchard, that some different soil should occur. Rocks beneath the ground, she thought, might account for it. The roots could have hit rock and not been allowed to flourish properly. She was just turning to leave when her eye fell on a small canvas bag. Thinking she had discovered some clue left by the intruders, she picked it up with great curiosity. It was heavy and jingled with pieces of metal. Opening it, she was stunned to see it held a quantity of guineas. Bobbie was off throwing apples at a tree. Delsie decided to keep her discovery a secret from the child. She concealed it under her pelisse, but was highly curious to get to her room and count the guineas. What could account for it? What sort of intruders came and took nothing, so far as she could see, but left a bag of gold worth a great deal?

"Shall we pick some of these pretty michaelmas daisies and marigolds before we go in?" she asked.

Together they went to the orchard's edge to gather these late-blooming flowers, before going inside for breakfast. They took them to their rooms to arrange in a vase. Once she achieved privacy, Delsie emptied the canvas bag on the counterpane, marveling at the quantity of gold pieces — one hundred in all. One hundred gold guineas — more than a year's salary. Her first inclination was to run to deVigne with the bag and ask his opinion, but Lady Jane was coming to call for her soon, and it would have to wait till after the shopping trip. Afraid to leave such a fortune in her room, where she was by no means sure it would be safe from prying eyes after her departure, she put it in her reticule and took it to the table with her. Miss Milne and Bobbie soon joined her. The three were in no hurry to dispatch their breakfast, but could not make it last till nine-thirty, at which time Lady Jane was to arrive. Bobbie was taken, unwilling, to the schoolroom for a lesson, while Mrs Grayshott sat going over her list, adding a new item at every spot where her eye fell. Beeswax and turpentine to remove the dust and grime from the saloon, more candles, a great deal of them as the house was so gloomy, embroidery woolens, and backing for her tambour frame. The items wanted seemed endless. She was still busy at this task when the knocker sounded. As Bristcombe was still invisible, she went herself to answer it. DeVigne stood at the door, his carriage waiting on the roadside.

"Good morning, cousin," he said brightly. "Still playing butler, I see. Did you speak to Bristcombe about leaving lights burning for you at night?"

"No, I spoke to his wife — but I never see him. I'm not sure I want to. Come in."

"He was in the orchard just now as I came along the road. I made sure you had set him to gather the withered apples. They won't be good for anything but pig feed, but I know your aversion to waste."

"I must speak to you," she said, ignoring this banter. She took him to the saloon, with a question as to why it was himself who had come in lieu of Lady Jane.

"We are to meet her in the village. With five of us, one carriage will not hold all your purchases on the return voyage, if you are the enthusiastic shopper most ladies are. I have business there, and shall bring Sir Harold back with me, leaving you three ladies to shop to your hearts' content. But surely that is not what you meant to ask me. From the size of your eyes, I hoped for missing knives or forks at the least."

"Nothing is missing," she said with an air of vast importance. "*Au contraire.*"

"You have found the vanishing linens?" he asked, taking up a seat on the sofa.

"Nothing so paltry. I have found a bag of gold!" she announced.

"Congratulations. Was it a *large* bag of gold?"

She fished it out from the bottom of her reticule and handed it to him. "It is one hundred guineas!" she said importantly.

"That should take care of the butcher," he said, hefting the bag, and shaking a couple of pieces out into his hand. "They seem genuine. Where did you find them?"

"You will think it incredible, but it's true! I found them under an apple tree in the orchard this morning. What *can* it mean?"

He looked at her, not at all so impressed as she had thought he would be with her find. "There haven't been any rainbows lately, so that cannot account for it — the pot of gold."

"Do be serious!"

"Perhaps Andrew, in one of those drunken ambulations you spoke of, dropped it one night, though I still can't credit he ever left the house, with Samson and Bristcombe here to watch him."

"They would not let him take so much money out with him in any case. What should I do? Ought I to advertise it, do you think? Oh, and I forgot to tell you, I know where it came from."

"An advertisement seems superfluous in that case," he suggested.

"Well it is not, because I don't know *who* was there, but *someone* was in the orchard last night very late, with a horse or horses. At least two men. I heard them talking."

"After you returned from the Hall?"

"Much later — not long before one o'clock, I think. I made sure it was only someone stealing the apples, and hardly gave it a thought, till I went into the orchard this morning and saw how far the fruit had deteriorated. Besides, it stands to reason anyone reduced to stealing half-rotten apples would not have a hundred guineas to lose."

"Are you quite sure you heard someone?"

"Absolutely. I am not at all imaginative. Bobbie heard them too. She thought it was the pixies." She sat thinking about it, then went on. "So it seems the pixies she was told about were not her papa in a drunken stupor after all. And *that*, you know, was the reason I held to account for her being put on the west side of the house, so she would not hear her father ranting about. DeVigne, is it possible there has been someone coming regularly into the orchard for years, ever since Bobbie was removed from the nursery? Only think, if they have been leaving bags of guineas for all that time, there must be a fortune about the house somewhere. I shall institute a search the moment I get back from the village."

"You do rather leap to conclusions. Still, it is mighty curious. In the orchard, eh? Let's have a look."

"It's no good. I went out bright and early, and couldn't find a single thing, except the bag of gold, that is. But what shall I do about it? I cannot keep it."

"Keep it for the time being. If it was lost by any innocent person, he won't be long coming to look for it."

"The horrid thought raises its head that innocent persons do not lurk about gardens and orchards that do not belong to them, carrying large sums of money. It must have been a criminal, and I know he will come back for it too. Have you heard any account of a robbery in the neighborhood?"

"No, nor can I conceive of any reason he should be in your orchard. Still, I'll inquire in the village this morning — discreetly. It will be best to keep this to ourselves."

"You *do* think there's something odd going on, don't you? Oh, what have you gotten me into?" she worried, wringing her hands.

"To date, the worst I have gotten you into is a bag of gold guineas. That should merit gratitude, not a scold. The only inconvenience to yourself has been a night's disturbed sleep. You make too much of it, cousin."

"Yes, a bag of gold belonging to some cutthroat burglar or smuggler, who will doubtless come after it in the night with a knife between his teeth. A mere bagatelle. I can't imagine why I tremble every time I think of it. I must put them somewhere for safekeeping. Will you take charge of them for me?"

"Not at all imaginative, you say?" he asked, with a quizzing smile. "The knife between the teeth, surely . . ." She stuffed the bag into his hands, for he had placed it on the sofa between them after examining it. "There is a vault in the study. Let us put it there — for the present."

When they went to this room, there was no key in the vault, so deVigne carried the money into town, in a pocket of his carriage. This was done surreptitiously to keep it from Bobbie, who went with them. The child regaled her uncle along the way with the story of the pixies, while the widow stared at him with an "I told you so" look.

Delsie felt very much like a princess from a fairy tale when she first wafted into the village inside the crested carriage, with every head turning toward it. The carriage stopped outside the Venetian Drapery Shoppe, the one good store in the village. It was frequented only by the gentry, as the articles within and, more particularly, their prices were beyond the range of mere working mortals. Delsie had occasionally entered to buy a bit of lace or ribbon, and to admire the larger items. Her real purchases were made at Bolton's, a less-elevated emporium across the street. She always felt she was encroaching to enter the former establishment. On her few forays, the salesman had looked down his nose at her and demanded in a supercilious tone if she wanted anything, or was "just looking." Today the same toplofty person was bowing and simpering, for deVigne had said at the carriage he would just step in with her and Bobbie and wait till Jane arrived.

"Mrs Grayshott will be opening an account here. Will you see she is taken care of?" was all he said. It was enough to set the clerk fawning on her in a manner that was every bit as jarring as his former neglect. His compliant voice was at her shoulder, pointing out a fine bit of imported lace, calling her attention to other wares. She was happy when Lady Jane arrived and told him they would take care of themselves. DeVigne then took his leave, and the two dames got down to rooting through the store in good earnest. They wanted first to obtain Bobbie's materials, as the child was pestering them on this point.

Lady Jane, an inveterate bargain-hunter, complained about the price of everything, in no low tone, and indeed her complaints seemed well taken. For the honor of residing on the shelves of the Venetian Drapery Shoppe instead of Bolton's, muslin was doubled in price. It was hastily decided between them that the more mundane purchases would wait for Bolton's, and only the luxuries be purchased here. And what luxuries there were! Silk stockings, the finest of crepes and velvets for gowns, laces, ribbons and buttons of unimagined splendor, every one a jewel. With Bobbie's materials selected, Delsie began the joyful task of choosing her own. She had intended having three new gowns made up for her role as Mrs Grayshott, but, with such a display of exotic goods before her, she could not limit herself to less than four — two afternoon outfits and two gowns for evening. The selection of accessories for the gowns too was pure pleasure. Mechlin lace, mother-of-pearl buttons, ribbons so narrow and dainty, a bottle of black bugle beads to decorate her finest gown. She began to wonder how they would transport all the purchases to the carriage, but discovered, before she exposed her ignorance, that they would be picked up by a footboy. There was no mention of paying. The bill would be sent. Then they were across the road to Bolton's. Here she had only Lady Jane to lend her consequence; she proved to be enough. On to the millinery shop for two delightful bonnets. How she regretted she was in mourning, but even a mourning bonnet, she discovered, could be flattering when one was willing to pay a small fortune for it. A black glazed straw with narrow black velvet ribbons lent her an unaccustomed dash, and a high poke bonnet too with a lifted brim would, as Jane practically pointed out, look well after she had put off her crepe.

It was half past one when they were through, and Delsie was beginning to think she would be very hungry indeed before she got back to the Cottage, but there was another delight in store for her. They repaired to the inn for luncheon, there to meet deVigne and Sir Harold. Delsie had partaken of an occasional repast there with her mama, on special occasions, but she had never before been shown to the best table, with half a dozen waiters nipping smartly about, filling glasses, and pressing a variety of dishes forward. It was a banquet. She was nearly as excited as Bobbie, who said happily that when she was grown up, she would eat all her meals at inns. "I *love* eating away from a house. Isn't it fun, Mama?"

"Great fun," Delsie agreed warmly, feeling as young and inexperienced as the child, and blushing when she saw deVigne regarding them with an amused smile.

She soon learned that in the view of the other adults, taking a meal at the inn was in the nature of a vile necessity. "I believe this is old mutton," Lady Jane complained, shoving it aside. "Pass that pigeon along, Max. Let us see if it is edible."

"This is a bad claret," Sir Harold, proclaimed, shaking his head sadly. "I would have done better to have an ale, like you, Max."

After dinner, Sir Harold and deVigne left in the former's carriage, and the ladies continued their shopping for household items now. "There is no reason you should be sunk to making such purchases as beeswax and turpentine yourself, Delsie, but that Mrs Bristcombe, you know — I doubt she has ever heard of them. We shall have this lot delivered. I don't plan to carry a jug of turpentine in a carriage with me. I like to get into the everything store from time to time. I find my servants will go on buying the same things forever, and never bother to try the new products. Now just take a look at this! Dr. Cropper's New Patching Cement, for mending broken china without leaving a trace. I threw out a very nice vase last week, only because the patching cement left yellow smears all over it, and when we tried to get them off, the vase fell apart in our hands. I'll try a bottle of this."

A great many fairly useless items of this sort were selected, before the ladies had their carriage called to return to the Cottage. Lady Jane entered, and over a cup of tea they proceeded to have their parcels brought in for a leisurely inspection, the most enjoyable part of any shopping spree, to compliment each other on their sagacity, and wonder whether the mother-of-pearl buttons bought at the Venetian Shoppe were not exact replicas of those seen at Bolton's at a fraction of the cost.

"Yes, I think we have paid double for the pleasure of having our buttons sewed onto a cardboard, instead of left in the box. Next time we shall know better," Delsie said.

It was pleasant to consider that such extravagant outings as this were now a part of one's life.

CHAPTER
EIGHT

While the ladies were still engaged at their happy, feminine task, deVigne came in unannounced. "I didn't bother to knock, fearing the butler would be tired from her shopping," he said.

"What is this?" Jane asked. "Delsie is surely not acting as her own butler. What is amiss with Bristcombe?"

"Mrs Grayshott's house is not yet in order," deVigne told her. "She has a severe servant problem. Do you happen to know what happened to Betsy Rose, Aunt? We can discover no servants in the house but the Bristcombes — and the governess, of course."

"She left a year ago, Betsy Rose," Jane answered promptly. "She got married to a local layabout. I made sure she had got herself a bad bargain, but have seen her since in the village looking fine as a star. A silken gown the hussy had on her back. Baggage."

"She must have nabbed herself a smuggler. The silken gown sounds like it. They bring in a good deal of silk here, as well as brandy," deVigne thought. "Andrew didn't replace her?"

"Lord only knows!" She threw up her hands. "I was here very little more than yourself, Max. Only to visit

Bobbie. I don't believe she ever was replaced. And are the Bristcombes jogging along with no help at all, then? No wonder the place is gone to rack and ruin. Still, I don't know what Bristcombe can be doing if he is not working inside the house, for it is clear as glass he hasn't touched the lawn or flowers."

"The apples were allowed to rot. They were not picked at all," Delsie added.

"This business must be settled at once," deVigne stated. "Can you recommend a couple of village girls for us, Jane? For maid's work."

Delsie felt the old familiar annoyance at being relegated to an onlooker in her own. life. "You forget, deVigne, *I* am more fully acquainted with the village girls than anyone else here. I have in mind a couple of my old students who will do very well. We had a few girls at the Parish School in the winter, when they were not needed at home for farm work."

"Sorry." He bowed his head to indicate his error. "I seem always to seek your approval for the wrong things. You will hire two girls yourself, then, I assume?"

"Certainly I shall. Did you put the ad in the paper about Mr Grayshott's debts?"

"Yes, and also inquired discreetly about any burglary in the village. There was none."

This last statement had to be explained to Lady Jane, who was thrown into a tizzy of delight at the unexpected finding of a bag of gold in one's orchard. She declared that she would run home that instant and have a look under her own trees. Her parcels were taken to her carriage by Lord deVigne, turned footman for the occasion. "My place for dinner tonight, Delsie," the dame called as she left. These reminders always raised a glow of happiness in the widow's bosom. It was so novel and pleasant an experience to belong to a family, and such a jolly, happy family too.

When she was gone, deVigne said, "Might this not be a good opportunity to discover the key of Andrew's vault? It must be looked into for the settling of his estate."

"Where should I begin to look? I haven't a notion where he would have kept it."

"Let's start with his desk."

They went to the study and looked through drawers, which yielded a welter of papers, but no keys. "Here is something — the receipt for the Bristcombes' wages for the last quarter of this year. He paid them two hundred and fifty pounds! You told me two hundred, deVigne."

"Servants *do* get an increase from time to time," he pointed out.

"Usually for improved service. They aren't worth half that."

"You are mentally comparing to your own salary as a teacher," he said, correctly.

"They got room and board as well."

"Along with all the sheets and towels they could carry off."

"You may laugh at me all you like. They are overpaid, and I *will* be rid of them."

"That is your affair. Now, about the keys — his bedroom very likely. He seldom left it the last few months."

"There is a table covered with medicine bottles and things just by his bed. It may be there." She excused herself and went to the room. She returned with not only the key, but another bag of gold.

"I found the key at the very back of the little drawer, hidden in a bottle under some pills," she explained.

"You're a sharp observer. How did you come to find it?"

"I pushed aside the papers — designs for some sort of an engine he had in mind, they looked like — and there was this one bottle. When I lifted it, it seemed very heavy, and then I saw the key, and at the very back of the drawer, this bag. It is just as I said. The pixies have been coming here for years and leaving bags of gold."

The bag was emptied and discovered to contain the same sum, one hundred guineas. One bag of gold deVigne could credit having become misplaced in the garden by accident; he had thought it was Andrew's entire savings, which he had somehow dropped in the garden while drunk, but two identical bags holding the same sum was more than coincidence,

"What the devil can this mean?" he asked, frowning.

"There are bound to be others around the house. Let us try if this is the key to the vault."

Without further ado it was tried, and it opened the vault, which was found to contain another ten of the canvas bags, each with what looked intriguingly like a hundred guineas, though they did not count them.

"Where did they come from? I don't understand!" the widow wailed, more chagrined than pleased to have this small fortune in her hands. No more did deVigne seem pleased.

"Could it be an income from some source, some investment?" she wondered. "He was used to be a partner in the shipyards, was he not?"

"He was the major owner. The Blewes Shipyard used to be the Grayshott Shipyard. He took Blewes in as junior partner when he married. When Andrew began drinking after Louise's death, Blewes gradually took over, becoming first senior partner, then later buying Andrew out entirely. Andrew foolishly put his money into unsound investments that went broke. He was always looking for a get-rich-quick scheme, instead of contenting himself with a good dividend. He blew the last of his money in setting up a small manufactory in Merton to produce a contrivance of his own invention. Some mechanical contraption to turn a spit it was, for roasting meat, you know. Quite clever, really, but it didn't catch on. He had no commercial enterprise going at the time of his death, however. I have been to see his solicitor. I can't imagine where this money could have been coming from. It is an utter mystery to me."

"I'll be arrested. I know it as surely as I am sitting here," she said resignedly. "You have married me to a thief! Oh, what shall I do with all this money?"

"I suggest you return it to the vault for the time being, and keep a close hand on the key. Here, take this bag you saddled me with too." He handed back the bag he had taken for her.

112

"Yes, you are eager to clean *your* hands of the evidence, and palm it all of on *me!*" she charged, accepting the bag gingerly, as though it were dirty, and stuffing it into the vault with the others. "That is twelve hundred guineas we have found today, and we haven't even begun to look about the house yet."

"He wouldn't have left it sitting around the place under plants or on window ledges. He wasn't *that* senile."

"Never mind trying to put a respectable face on it, calling it senility. He was an alcoholic, which is much worse. I shall have a good look around as soon as you have left."

"Is that an oblique hint for me to leave, and without a glass of Andrew's excellent brandy to prepare me for the cold winds of December?" deVigne inquired.

"I hope I am not so uncivil. Let us go into the saloon, where I endeavor to keep a few twigs smoldering to ward off the worst of the weather."

DeVigne went to kick the few logs into flames, while the widow fetched the decanter and one glass. She had no taste for the strong beverage. When she returned, deVigne sat very much at his ease, fingering a bolt of black crepe she had bought that morning.

"Thank you," he said, accepting the glass, "May I make a suggestion? I cannot speak for others, but for myself, I like a very small glass of brandy, not a brimming vessel; I can't drink the half of this, and it is a shame to waste it. He carefully tossed half a glass into the fire, where it flared into leaping flames, blue and green.

"How lovely!" Delsie exclaimed, smiling at the show. "Now I know something useful to do with that dreadful drink."

"Wastrel! If you discover a hogshead of the stuff you don't want, I'll take it off your hands." He turned back to the materials on the sofa beside him. "Pity you must be confined to black for a year. You would look well in brighter colors," he mentioned, examining her face, as though selecting his preferred shade.

She felt a sudden warmth at the personal tone the conversation was taking. "I am used to black," she answered dampingly.

"I have never seen you in anything but dark colors."

"I didn't begin wearing black till after my mother's death. I was obliged to dress somberly when I worked at St Mary's. Now, of course, I am a widow, and when they put me in Bridewell for possessing stolen money, I daresay I shall have to wear black there too."

"I shall use my influence to have you transported if you prefer it, ma'am," he offered kindly.

"I knew I might depend on you to do the right thing by me, so caring as you have been for my every comfort! Pray make it America, and not Australia. I think I would prefer even wild Indians to the sultry climate that prevails in the latter."

"You may be sure I shall do all in my power to ease your shipment to America. Plead for the widow, like the Good Book says. I'll see if I can't get you isolated from the murderers and the less desirable of the criminal element. But seriously, where could he regularly steal such a sum? One would think even the most simple-minded of victims would tumble to it after a couple of times, and take some precautions to prevent ten or twelve repetitions."

"What was the one bag doing in the *orchard*, that is what *I* cannot fathom."

"Right in the orchard was it, or at the edge?"

"In the middle, under one of those little runted trees. Why are those two smaller than the others? Do you know?"

"I believe Sir Harold told me, after I returned from a season in London one year, that two trees had died, and Andrew replaced them. It is not unusual to lose a tree. I have a couple of smaller ones in my own orchard, but they never produce gold, only apples."

"If that ingenious husband of mine has invented a means of turning apples to gold, it is a pity the secret died with him. Bobbie calls them the pixie trees, and says they are more valuable than all the others put together. Is it usual for a smaller tree to have a better yield?"

"No, it is some nonsense they've been filling her head with. I wouldn't encourage her to believe that ignorant sort of superstition."

Again the widow bristled. "*I* have not been filling her head with superstition, milord. It is Mrs Bristcombe. I am trying to discourage the idea of pixies."

"Sorry again, cousin. Why is it I invariably raise your hackles? — and I am fairly walking on eggs, too. You are very sensitive, I think?"

"Perhaps it is rather that *you* are insensitive," she replied, and felt she had gained a point, though it was a somewhat arbitrary charge.

"Let us hope that under your tutelage I shall become more finely attuned to your sensibilities, ma'am. Jane is kind enough to tell me I am a biddable fellow, and we are all, we bachelors, more amenable to being led by a pretty young lady than anyone else." Delsie's eyes widened at this leading statement, but before she could give voice to any objection, he spoke on calmly. "No, don't try to quell me with one of your schoolteacher's scowls. I have been out of the schoolroom a good many years. And never had such a delightful tutor when I was in it either," he finished with a little suggestion of a smile. Then he immediately arose. "I have a distinct sensation I should take my leave, before the teacher brings out her ruler to slap my knuckles."

As he entered the hallway, Bristcombe lounged in through the front door, wearing shabby clothing and with his face not shaved.

"Ah, the mysterious vanishing butler!" deVigne said ironically, raking the man from head to toe, his eyes lingering on the incipient beard, the muddied boots. "Mrs Grayshott has been wondering where you keep yourself these days, Bristcombe. When a lady pays a good sum for a servant's time, she expects him to perform his duties. You do not appear to serve as a butler in this establishment. At least one *hopes* it was not your intention to show me the door in that getup. From the jungle at the front door it is clear you have not turned gardener. May one inquire how you *do* manage to fill your days?"

"I've been getting wood," he said, though he carried no wood with him.

"Mrs Grayshott will be happy to hear it. While we catch a glimpse of you, there are a few points that want mentioning. You will leave lights burning for Mrs Grayshott when she is out in the evenings, and remain up and about till she is safely returned, after which you will lock up carefully. Do you understand?" he asked, in a polite tone that carried an unmistakable threat.

"Yes, milord," Bristcombe mumbled sulkily.

"Good. Otherwise it will be necessary to find servants who know their duties."

DeVigne was not chided by so much as a glance for his interference on this occasion. Delsie was happy to have the unpleasant task of a scolding done for her. DeVigne took his leave, and Bristcombe came into the saloon after Mrs Grayshott.

"Begging your pardon, Mrs Grayshott, but me and the missus would like to go visiting my folks tomorrow. Just five miles down the road past the village. Sunday was our regular day off when the master was alive."

"By all means, go ahead." And what a relief to be rid of you, she added to herself.

"We'll go after your luncheon and be back by dark, or soon after. I'll be here to lock up for the night, and leave the lights on for you and all," he added in quite a humble tone.

She was half pleased and half angered that the baron's brief lecture to Bristcombe had proved so efficacious, when she had been wrangling to less avail with the wife for two days. She took her purchases upstairs and spent an agreeable hour going through fashion books choosing patterns for her new gowns. Next she went to the escritoire and wrote the notes to the village girls she wished to come to her. She would send them into the village with a servant. The recipients would not appreciate having to frank them. This done, she began sorting through the desk to discard those items belonging to her predecessor that were now useless. She debated for five minutes whether to keep or discard the printed stationery bearing the name Mrs Grayshott. Her inclination was to throw it into the grate and burn it up as fast as she could, so much did she dislike the name, but in the end thrift overcame inclination, and she kept it for rough notes and lists. As she reassembled the drawers to her own convenience, she recalled Bobbie mentioning a secret panel at the back of one. Worked with a button, she had said. She examined drawers for buttons, and found, cleverly concealed on the underside of the top drawer, a little button. When she pushed it, a soft click was heard, and the back panel of the drawer fell forward to reveal another canvas bag. "Oh, no!" she moaned softly to herself, pulling it out. No counting was necessary. She was becoming very familiar with the weight of a hundred gold guineas.

CHAPTER
NINE

News of her latest discovery was brought to her relatives as soon as she was seated in Lady Jane's cozy saloon with a glass of sherry in her hand that evening. Jane was enthralled, and confirmed on the spot she would go to the Cottage the very next day to help her conduct a thorough search, from attics to cellars.

"From attic to kitchens," Delsie corrected. "Any gold stashed in the cellars may remain there."

"My dear, that is the likeliest place to have put it," Jane pointed out.

"I saw black beetles in the kitchen. There would certainly be rats in the cellars. I shan't go near them," she stated firmly.

"I have been looking for an excuse to get into Andrew's cellars," deVigne claimed. "If he has a hogshead of that brandy you like to throw on the fire, I shall take it as my fee for looking for gold."

"Agreed!" Mrs Grayshott declared. "And it was you who threw it on the fire," she added.

"Brandy will not put out a fire," Sir Harold informed them.

His spouse repressed the urge to tell him to shut up, and said instead, "It is odd finding one of the bags in

Louise's desk. Do you think she put it there? That Andrew has been acting this way for so long?"

"There is no way we shall discover it now," her nephew replied.

"Is it possible he had more money than you knew?" Delsie asked. "You mentioned he lost a good deal in poor investments, but might he not have kept some cash on hand, in the house?"

"I can't think so. He was eager to get his hands on Louise's settlement in cash, and told me at the time he was in tight waters financially. That was three years ago, more or less, for he went through his roll very quickly after Louise died. Went on a big binge of selling everything. In fact, he sold his own yacht to settle some accounts. You recall he had kept the *Robert-Lou* for his own use, Jane?" deVigne asked.

"Yes. When he sold out to Blewes, he kept the smallest ship and fitted it up for a pleasure craft. Too big, of course, and I don't believe he had it out above two or three times. It was foolish to keep it. Well, it required a crew of six or seven men, and Andrew himself never was much of a sailor. It was a sentimental gesture, keeping it and naming it for his wife and daughter. He sold it to some fellow in Merton, I think."

"His own uncle took it off his hands. Old Clancy it is who has the *Robert-Lou*," Sir Harold told them.

"I wish I could remember . . ." Delsie said, staring into the leaping flames. Everyone looked at her to hear an explanation of this pregnant statement. She went on: "During those few very brief conversations I had with

120

Mr Grayshott, just before and after the ceremony, he talked about money."

"I made sure he was wooing you," Lady Jane laughed.

"No, he asked me to take good care of Roberta, then said something to the effect that I would be rewarded for it. He mentioned that Louise's portion and the Cottage were for Bobbie, but said *he* had some money — something of the sort."

"His personal effects were left to you — in fact, in the will the wording is that his estate entire is bequeathed to his wife," deVigne outlined. "It is no fortune — some few pieces of jewelry, his horses and carriages, his patents, which I think he still, at the end, believed might be worth something."

"The spit was a clever idea," Lady Jane suggested. "For some people still use a dog in a wheel to turn the spit, you know, and it is disgusting to think of having a dirty old dog in the kitchen."

"He never could peddle the hundred or so he made up," deVigne reminded her. "About the horses and carriages, cousin, you would be well advised to sell them. I don't hesitate to make the suggestion, as the hunters are a man's high-bred goers, and the sporting carriage is an extremely precarious high-perch phaeton."

"Yes, and the traveling carriage is a great lumbering coach a hundred or so years old, not useful at all," Lady Jane added. "Every strap on it would break if anyone sat inside, I am convinced."

"What happened to Louise's silver, the art collection, all that fine furniture?" Sir Harold demanded petulantly.

"That was all gone years ago, my dear," his wife told him, with scanty patience. She had listened to him rant for two months when the sale had taken place.

"Andrew used to have a fine residence in Merton," deVigne explained aside to his widow. "The Cottage was never intended for more than a summer residence, to allow them to bring their family home and still have some privacy. Andrew and I never did rub along very congenially, as I originally made some efforts to dissuade her from accepting him. The Merton place was sold off some years ago."

"You think these bags of gold I keep finding come after that date, then?"

"It is difficult to believe Andrew would have parted with his patrimony — and his yacht, which he loved — if he had had a fortune sitting around in gold. It must have been acquired since that time."

"He was into some illegal business. That is the only explanation," Sir Harold assured them. "Never liked the fellow above half. Don't see why you let your sister have him, Max."

"He seemed a rising young gent at the time. The best of a bad lot, for some of his family are hardly presentable. As to *letting* Louise do anything, you forget, Harold, what a hothead she was. She paid very little attention to the commands of a younger brother, and with her fortune in her own hands, she would have certainly dashed off and married him if I had forbidden the match."

"Give the devil his due; he made Louise a good husband. Till her death he was a proper gentleman,"

Jane reminded them. "It was losing her, so devoted to her as he was, that turned him to drink, and the drink accounts for the rest of it. Well, the drink and lack of breeding, for a real gentleman would not have gone to pieces only at losing a wife."

"He was beginning to drink pretty heavily before Louise's death," deVigne mentioned, "but she kept him under some control."

"So no one knows how to account for the gold?" Mrs Grayshott asked, to call them back to order.

No one had a sensible suggestion on the subject, so they turned to other topics, deVigne to inquire of Mrs Grayshott whether she had contacted the village girls, and what she would like done with the carriages and horses. It was agreed he would take them to auction, and suggested that he would be happy to look about for some replacement more suitable to a lady's needs. Lady Jane was caught by her husband to hear a lengthy exposition of the many historical atrocities committed in the lust for gold. To escape him, she asked Delsie how the governess performed her duties.

"She is an excellent girl, well informed and conscientious. I enjoy her company, but to cut expenses I had thought I might teach Bobbie myself. It would be one less servant to pay, and I am qualified to undertake her training."

"Oh, my dear, don't think of it!" Jane expostulated at once. "If you haven't someone to look after Bobbie, you will have a child on your hands twenty-four hours a day. You would be tied leg and wing, not a minute free to receive callers or to make a call yourself, or to come to us in the evenings, for you would not want to leave her in Mrs Bristcombe's charge, I am convinced. She would frighten the child with her stories of pixies and other superstitious ignorance. You cannot dispense with a woman of some sort to look after the child."

These disadvantages had already occurred to the widow. She was fond of Roberta, but knew as well that a lady in her new circumstances was not saddled full-time with her children. "The reason I married Mr Grayshott was to look after Roberta," she reminded them.

"You *are* looking after her," deVigne added protest. "You are her legal guardian, and taking your job of husbanding her monies very seriously, but it is nonsense to speak of dispensing with a governess. As you settle into a more regular sort of a life here, you will find you haven't time to devote your whole day to the child. That was never our intention. Even as a schoolmistress, you were not on duty twenty-four hours a day. I will risk giving you an unsolicited piece of advice. Keep the governess if you feel she is competent, and replace her if you feel otherwise. How does Bobbie like her?"

"They are on good terms, but . . ."

"Keep her, then," Jane said conclusively. "Besides, I am the one who got Miss Milne the position, and she needs it. The father is dead, and there are three girls at home. It would be cruel to turn her off for no reason."

This cunning fabrication, making an unexceptionable reason for Mrs Grayshott to retain the girl, succeeded very well. There was no more talk of being rid of Miss Milne.

Dinner was called, and a peaceful evening was whiled away over a few hands of whist. As Mrs Grayshott put on her bonnet and pelisse to leave, Lady Jane reminded her they would have a treasure hunt on the morrow, the details to be set up after church the next morning. When deVigne drove Delsie home to the Cottage, he inquired into her statement that Andrew had said he had money — had he specified in what form, or how much, or where?

"No, it was very odd. I thought so at the time, and attributed it to his weak condition. He just said he had some money, that he had saved it — I don't recall exactly, I was so confused myself. I think he was trying to tell me where it was, when you came in."

"This must be what he meant, the bags of guineas. Perhaps he received some small inheritance from a relative. I heard nothing of it, but it is possible, in which case the mysterious bags of guineas are your own. He left his estate to you."

"I have the sinking apprehension they were not bequeathed to him by any kindly relative. I think Sir Harold is right, and he was involved in some illegal business. Am I in any way responsible for my husband's crimes in the eyes of the law, I wonder?"

"Don't be foolish, cousin. If your husband was indeed participating in anything illegal, it has nothing to do with you."

"Receiving stolen money has to do with me. Why, I am no less than an accessory after the fact. I shall end up in the stocks, with my former pupils pelting stones at me."

"This is absurd," he said brusquely. "It was all done before your time, and without your knowledge. There is no way it can possibly involve you."

"Fine talk, but you are not a lawyer. I daresay I shall have need of one before this mess is settled."

"Let us wait till we have conducted a search of the house tomorrow. If we *do* find any considerable sum of money, we shall have to look into how he came by it. Until that time, I shouldn't worry my head about it unduly."

"The thirteen hundred already found seems a considerable sum to *me*!" she objected. "I don't know how you expect me to go to bed and listen to the pixies playing in the orchard as if nothing had happened. If I am lucky, I shall find another bag of gold tomorrow, to add to my ill-gotten gains. I wish I were back at Miss Frisk's and St Mary's School," she said glumly.

"Do you indeed regret your marriage?" he asked, with a serious note in his voice. "You seem to me happier than you were used to be. I recall seeing you on the streets in the village, always whisking by at a great rate with a frown on your face, or in church on Sunday, looking as sober as a judge. That cannot have been a carefree life for you either."

"I did not have a frown on my face!"

"I never saw you smile till after your marriage."

"You never looked," she answered swiftly. "If you had, you could not have seen my face for the dust your carriage kicked up, bowling past at fifteen miles an hour."

"I didn't drive my carriage into church."

"No one smiles and laughs in church. It would be unseemly."

"You are avoiding the issue, cousin. Do you truly regret this marriage I foisted on you?"

"I regret the bags of guineas," she evaded. As she considered the change in her life, she could not keep up any pretense of regretting the rest of it. "Of course I like Bobbie," she added, as a sop.

The carriage swept up to the door of the Cottage. As he helped her to alight, he said, "Lucky Bobbie! I see Bristcombe has a light burning for you. I'll have a look around the orchard before I leave."

"The pixies don't arrive till twelve-thirty or one. You will only muddy your shoes for nothing, going there now."

"If you hear anything in the night, don't take it into your head to go and investigate it yourself. You can call Bristcombe, or tell me tomorrow and we'll set up a watch."

"That warning was unnecessary. I am not quite the daring creature you take me for. I shall pull the covers over my head, or run into Bobbie's room for protection."

"I have already said 'lucky Bobbie,' have I not? Good night, cousin. Pleasant dreams." He opened the door for her to enter and closed it after her, leaving the astonished widow in the hallway with a startled question on her face.

CHAPTER
TEN

Bristcombe was not in the hallway waiting for her, but as Delsie mounted the stairs, she heard him come up from the kitchen and lock the front door. Abovestairs lights were left burning as well, and she called down to him that she would take care of them to save his coming up. Looking in on Bobbie upon her return from dinner was becoming a habit, as was the tender emotion she felt to see that innocent face, vulnerable in sleep. My *daughter*, she thought! Only a stepdaughter really, but mine. It was an awesome responsibility she had shouldered, with very little thought to the child, but only to herself, her own troubles and of course her gain. She was a responsible woman, however, and had no thought of trying to avoid the responsibility. She welcomed it, in fact. Life would be futile with no responsibility, empty with no one to love. Already she was coming to love her new family.

These were her warm thoughts as she prepared for bed, still with her as she put out her lamp and tried to sleep. The little snake in this new Eden was the mysterious business in the orchard, and the unwanted gold. She listened for sounds of intrusion from beyond her window and heard none. She had not been in bed long enough to be near sleep when she heard the noise, sharp and close by. It was beneath her window — there where the French doors of the study opened onto a small shelled area that had once served as an outdoor conversation corner, before the shrubbery had encroached. It was a distinct rattling sound, as of a garden implement being knocked over or dropped. She was out of bed in a flash, looking through the window. A tattered shred of cloud partly obscured the hazy moon, but there was enough light to make out a dark form bending over and picking up whatever he had knocked down. Her heart pounded with fear. Good God! Were they planning to break right into the house this time? She should rouse Bristcombe. This hardly seemed preferable to facing the invader alone. She watched, tense, to see if the man — there was only one visible this time, nor had she heard anything to indicate the presence of animals — tried to gain entry. He did not. He backed into the shadows, no longer in her view, but she knew he was there, waiting, while she waited and observed above. Then he left — just walked away, around the corner to the back of the house.

If he tried to enter by that means, Bristcombe would certainly hear him. The Bristcombes slept in a room off the kitchen. She was suddenly seized by an idea that was either madness or inspiration, she hardly knew which. Maybe the Bristcombes were in on it, whatever was going on. In a flash, the idea had gained control of her mind. The Bristcombes, that unsavory pair, were up to something. The woman trying to be rid of her, and the man never where he should be, or doing what he was paid to. They were using Bobbie's house for some criminal activity. She must find out what it was. It would be dangerous, but there in the next room her innocent responsibility lay sleeping, at the mercy of these people. She squared her shoulders, slipped on her robe, shuffled into mules, and went to the door of her chamber. Her courage took a deep plunge there at the doorway to the dark corridor. What if they had guns, knives . . .?

She was dreadfully aware of her inability to deal with even one of the evildoers, if it should be one of the Bristcombes. What if there was a group? Miss Milne's doorway was only a step beyond Bobbie's. She ducked in and shook the girl's arm. She wouldn't ask her to come downstairs, but just let her know she was going in case . . . in case she didn't come back. Hardly a reassuring thought. And if the girl *insisted* on coming along, that was quite her own affair. To Miss Milne's credit and Delsie's infinite relief, the governess insisted on accompanying her mistress.

"I woke up all of a sudden, ma'am, and thought I heard something fall over down below. A clattering sound it was, like a shovel or rake," the girl said, perfectly wide-awake. "I didn't bother getting up to have a look. There was only the one man, you say?"

"Yes, I saw only one."

"I wonder who it could be? I'll go down with you, and we'll each take a poker for our defense." Miss Milne went in the dark and took up her own weapon, while Mrs Grayshott decided to have one from the saloon below. Without any candle to betray their

130

presence, they huddled together down the stairs, tiptoeing and clinging to each other's arm. All was silent, and dark, and extremely frightening. They crept to the French doors that were beneath Mrs Grayshott's window, stood with their pokers at the ready, staring into the black night, seeing nothing more treacherous than the naked black branches of trees, swaying against skies hardly less black.

"I'll just open the door and listen a moment," Mrs Grayshott said. This met with no disapproval, and it was done. A somewhat eerie moaning of the low wind through the bare trees was added to their discomfort, as was a piercingly cold breeze. For two minutes they both listened, ears on the stretch, till they were convinced the intruder was gone, at which point Miss Milne mentioned wondering what had been knocked over.

"It can't have been more than a step away. I'll slip out and have a look," Mrs Grayshott decided. This was only half her reason. What she truly wished to see was whether any more bags of guineas had been dropped.

"I'll go with you," Miss Milne offered at once. Really, she was a perfect governess, becoming more valuable and less dispensable by the second. But still, a Miss Milne at the doorway was as good protection as one at her elbow, seeing what (if anything) was picked up.

"Wait here. I won't be a minute," Mrs Grayshott told her, and went alone out the door. "It's a shovel," she called back over her shoulder in a low voice as she discerned in the darkness the outline of one leaning against the side of the house.

"I wonder if he was digging something," Miss Milne called back in a whisper.

"I'll have a look while I'm here." With eyes becoming accustomed to the gloom, the details of the night scene were becoming more easily recognizable.

"Be careful!" Miss Milne cautioned, coming to put her head out the French door for purposes of surveillance.

Delsie walked silently the few yards to the back of the building, looking about for any signs of either dropped canvas bags, or possibly freshly-dug holes, finding neither. A sudden keening gust of wind made her realize the folly of continuing the search in the middle of a black December night, wearing only a robe. She'd be lucky if she didn't catch a cold as a result of this stunt. Just before returning to the French doors, she took a quick peep around the corner that gave a view of the back of the Cottage. She nearly fainted from shock. There, hiding in the shadows less than a yard away, stood the man, dressed all in black, his face a white blur, as he flattened himself against the wall. Some stifled sound of terror was in her throat. She tried to run, and discovered that, as in some nightmare, her limbs were frozen. Flight was impossible. She just stood, straining her eyes in the darkness at the man, who was staring back at her.

The man recovered his wits first. His arms shot out, suddenly, swiftly, and his hands grabbed her wrists, jerking her around the corner. They were very strong

132

hands. The lurching movement pulled her against him, where she could feel the brush of his jacket against her cheek. In a fog of absolute panic, she struggled to be free, pushing against his chest, catching some small metallic object that dangled from a pocket. His hands held firm. Suddenly one hand released its hold and the arm went around her waist. Before she had time to even wonder what was happening, his head came down and his lips found hers. She was being soundly kissed, with the man's two arms around her now, holding her in an unbreakable grasp. It was a bizarre incident. It should have been horrifying as well, but her horror was not so strong as she would have thought. His cheeks were smooth; his embrace, while unwanted and in fact savage, sent a thrill through her. As a host of sensations jumbled through her brain, there emerged in the midst of them the thought that the man was a gentleman. This was patent nonsense. He was a criminal, but he was a clean-shaven criminal at least, not a dirty, rough, repulsive man.

As quickly as he had grabbed her, she was released. The man turned and disappeared into the night. Delsie became aware suddenly of the chilly night air, and of the softly calling voice of her companion behind her. "Are you all right, ma'am? What's happened?" Miss Milne asked anxiously. "Did he hurt you?"

The unexpected reaction was a definite feeling of pique that Miss Milne had seen the embrace. "No. That is — you saw what happened."

"He was kissing you, the bold creature! Who could it have been?"

"Let us go inside. I'm freezing." They hastened their steps back into the saloon. "I've no idea who it could be."

"It looked like . . . but that's impossible. He'd never behave so shamelessly," Miss Milne said, chattering excitedly.

"Did you recognize the man?"

"Oh, no! I couldn't see a thing but an outline."

"You said it looked like someone. Who did you mean?"

"It was the size of Lord deVigne was what I thought, and wearing evening clothes too. I saw the white shirt against the black coat, and there aren't many gentlemen hereabouts. But of course it could not have been him," Miss Milne stated confidently.

"I should think not, indeed," the widow said primly. Then together the two remounted the stairs, parting at the governess's door with a few words as to not mentioning this incident to Bobbie.

"There's one thing we're sure of anyway, ma'am," Miss Milne said. "It wasn't Mr Bristcombe, dressed up so fine. I wonder who it can have been." Her voice sounded a little wistful.

When she was safely back in her own warm bed once more, the widow was forced to admit that she too had been struck with the thought that it was Lord deVigne who had kissed her. She puzzled over this. The height was right, the clothing, the feel of it indicating a good quality, though she had not herself discerned that the man wore an evening suit. She knew deVigne had worn one that evening, just an hour before, when he had

134

brought her home. And that little metal watch fob she had felt hanging from the man's waistcoat pocket — it could have been a golden wishbone. Indeed, it was hard to conceive what else it could possibly have been — two little prongs she had felt between her fingers. And he had worn that fob tonight. She had particularly noticed he had the habit of fingering it unconsciously when he spoke.

Why should Lord deVigne be skulking about the yard at an hour past midnight? Why indeed, when she had told him less than twenty-four hours before that men had been there. He might have been looking for them, trying to discover who they were, and what they were doing. It was entirely possible he had been there. The likeliest thing was that he had sent his carriage home without him and had stayed behind, so little time had passed between her entering the house and the sound outside. He had even mentioned having a look around. Of course it had been deVigne, which gave rise to the next question. Why had he kissed her? He had not, to her knowledge, the reputation of a flirt. His name was never linked with any of the village girls. Such a juicy bit of gossip would have been passed along by Miss Frisk. The riddle kept her awake for the better part of an hour. Before she slept, she was concerned too for how she should act when next they met, whether she should drop a hint of her suspicions. She thought she would not. It could not be other than extremely embarrassing. DeVigne was impervious to such trifling matters — he never reacted to anything. It would be herself who ended up with a scarlet face, feeling a fool for *his* misbehavior. Best to say nothing and hope he would have the grace to do likewise. If it had actually been deVigne, that is. And what if it hadn't?

This was a new puzzle, one that required a fresher head than hers. She was nodding off to sleep.

CHAPTER
ELEVEN

Delsie awoke in the morning to her troubling memories, and to lead-gray skies, from which a cold rain streaked down. It was Sunday. Rain had never deterred her from attending church when she had had to walk, and it did not occur to her that it would be a reason when there were carriages to transport her. She dressed in her black gown before joining Bobbie and Miss Milne to descend to the breakfast table. In an effort to enroll herself in her mistress's good books, Mrs Bristcombe actually attempted a smile when she served the meal. Her wide girth was encased in a clean white apron, and her hair had been brushed. Taking these changes for tokens of obedience, Delsie said, "You and your husband have a bad day for your visit, Mrs Bristcombe. It is a pity."

"It may let up by noon," the dame answered, still smiling. The widow's surprise was great when the woman next asked in quite a civil tone if there was any errand she could do while passing through the village. Delsie first said no, then changed her mind and gave her the letters to her former pupils to whom she was offering positions. She even condescended to tell her housekeeper the contents of the letters, assuring her that the girls were good, reliable workers, who would be a help to her. She thought the smile on Mrs Bristcombe's face wore a different character than before, but it was so new a sight to see any upturning of the woman's lips that she could not be sure.

"I'll deliver them for you. Right on my way," she said agreeably, and waddled from the room.

"We shall wear our new bonnets, even if it is raining," Delsie said to Roberta. "We can take an umbrella." She wished to have some visible sign of her new status on this first trip up the aisle of the local church.

"We don't go to church when it rains," Bobbie stated simply.

Roberta seldom attended at all. Delsie tried to remember whether the others stayed away when the weather was bad. They were frequently absent, but they were sociable, often away visiting or in London, and she could not be certain Bobbie was correct. She made her own preparations to attend in any case, then went below to sit in the saloon and wait. Church began at eleven. She watched as the hands of the clock showed her ten-thirty, ten forty-five, ten-fifty, at which time she put aside her bonnet. Clearly there would be no church for her today. Before she had decided what to do, there was a knock on the front door. Bristcombe came to tell her deVigne's carriage was waiting. It was too late. They would miss half the service. With a *tsk* of annoyance she hastened to the door herself, to give deVigne a gentle hint that a half-hour drive should be begun at least thirty minutes before the function was to begin. There was only a footman at the door. A glance beyond showed her a perfectly empty carriage.

"Sorry we're late, ma'am. The master don't go to church when it pours so. He didn't think to send the carriage to see if you'd like to attend, till just a minute ago."

"Pray thank Lord deVigne, but I do not plan to attend either when it has got so late," she answered coldly, then went back into the saloon, miffed. The next preoccupation was how to pass the morning indoors, for the rain made going out impossible. She was eager to begin searching in earnest for further stores of hidden canvas bags. Lady Jane was not there to join her, but she would start anyway. Mr Grayshott's room seemed a likely spot.

"I told you we don't go to church when it rains," Bobbie danced out the door to inform her as she passed down the hall. "I don't have to study on Sunday either. What shall we do, Mama?"

"We are going to tidy up your papa's room," she told the child, who dangled along happily at her heels. She would say nothing about the money if she found any, but set it aside for concealing in the vault later.

"It certainly is untidy, isn't it?" Bobbie asked her.

The room had become Mr Grayshott's main living quarters during the last few months, and was cluttered with personal objects. Books, cards, games, old papers, and magazines abounded, littering every surface. No dusting or cleaning appeared to have been done since his death, or some weeks preceding it, by the quantity of dust everywhere.

She looked systematically through the dresser, the clothes-press, the night table, under the bed, explaining to Bobbie that she was looking for dust.

"There's lots of it under the bed," Bobbie pointed out.

"Indeed there is. I shall be sure to tell the maids about it when they come. We are getting two girls from the village to help us. You will like them — young, jolly girls."

With a sigh and a last look about the room, she concluded there was no hidden wealth here. Then it occurred to her that a well-established place for hiding things was under the mattress. She was just considering how to hide any possible find from Bobbie when the governess tapped at the door.

"There's a message from Lady Jane, ma'am," she said. "She'd like you to take Miss Roberta to her this afternoon after luncheon to spend the afternoon and stay to dinner. She doesn't go out herself in the damp because of her joints aching. Shall I tidy her up? It's nearly time for luncheon."

"Yes, thank you. Oh, and Miss Milne, as the Bristcombes are leaving this afternoon, you might like to come with us. You will not want to stay here all alone."

"I was going to suggest it, ma'am. My cousin Betsy works at the Dower House, and I thought I might have a wee visit with her."

"Excellent. You can come in the carriage that will be sent for us."

"Thank you, Mrs Grayshott."

140

She took Roberta away. Delsie quietly closed the door after them before tipping back the mattress. Mr Grayshott had liked his comfort. A soft, bulging feather tick rested on top of the firmer straw-filled one. Removing them posed a difficult problem. The feather tick she finally managed to push off, listening closely for the telltale tinkle of coins from within. There was none. The firmer straw-filled one was more difficult to remove. In order to be rid of it, it was necessary to shove it aside, then climb up on the springs to complete the job. She was panting with the effort, and lay back a moment to rest. Casting up her eyes, she saw that the canopy sagged unevenly in the center, as though some weight bore on it. Her heart quickening, she leapt from the bed, dragged a chair to allow her a better view, and saw a whole heap of the canvas bags. She reached in for them, pulling them down and tossing them on the bed, one by one, counting each. There were an even dozen. Another twelve hundred stolen guineas! The feeling that settled over her was close to gloom. Was there no end to it? Was every nook and cranny of the house to yield more evidence of criminality on her husband's part?

She clambered down, felt under the straw mattress from both sides instead of trying to remove it completely, and satisfied herself that she had got them all. The feather tick was returned, then she went like a thief with her twelve bags down to her own room. Better secrete them in the vault. She wrapped them up in her pelisse to conceal them from the eyes of the Bristcombes, should they be skulking below. With trembling fingers, she shoved them into the vault, which would hardly hold such a cache. If she found any more, she would have to discover a new hiding place. She felt as guilty as if she had stolen them herself.

Her upset continued throughout luncheon. She could hardly eat a bite, listened with only half an ear to Bobbie's excited chatter about visiting Aunt Jane. The discovery even wiped from her mind the preceding night's episode, which had been much with her throughout the morning. It was deVigne who came to take them to the Dower House in his carriage. With Miss Milne and Roberta present, the news could not be relayed to him. She regarded him surreptitiously, trying to read whether he was showing any discomfort or guilt over last night. He looked impassive, as ever. It seemed suddenly impossible to credit that it had been he. Any number of gentlemen possessed an evening suit. The watch fob need not have been a wishbone. It might have been any small object. He suddenly spoke, interrupting her line of thought.

"I'm sorry if I caused you to miss church this morning. I don't know whether it is your custom to attend in such inclement weather. It is not my own, but I know you are fond of church. I didn't think of it till too late, I'm afraid."

"Yes, I always attend church on Sunday. I used to walk in the rain, and should certainly have gone had the carriage been there on time. But I hope by next week I shall not have to trouble you, deVigne. I hope to set up my own gig as soon as you manage to sell Mr Grayshott's carriages and horses."

"*Gig?*" he asked, in a loud voice.

"Yes, gig," she answered firmly. There would clearly be an argument over this point, but, like the new discovery of money, it must await more privacy.

"The Bristcombes have got a gig," Bobbie announced. "I like it. It's so nice and jiggly."

The rain had let up during the morning, and a weak ray of sunlight was attempting to force its way through the curtain of lingering mist. Bobbie was taken into the saloon and made a fuss over by her great aunt, while Miss Milne went to visit with her cousin. The family business could not be discussed in front of Bobbie. Lady Jane soon surmised from the impatient movements of Mrs Grayshott that there was news to be relayed, and said after half an hour, "You'll never guess what cook is doing, Bobbie. Making gingerbread. Would you like to pop down to the kitchen and help?" Indeed she would, and scampered off in high spirits.

"What a treasure that child is," Jane said fondly, "but, as we mentioned t'other day, one cannot forever have the children present. I know you have something to tell, Delsie, and have been on thorns this thirty minutes to hear it. Do tell me, have you had your search without me, and found more gold?"

"Twelve bags!" she exclaimed, unable to hold in the news another moment. She outlined amidst excited questions the details of her find. "And you may be sure that is not the end of it."

"We must definitely go over the whole place tomorrow," Jane declared, her eyes shining with eager anticipation.

"I have been doing a little peeking here and there. I think the saloon is clean — of *money*, I mean, for of course it is filthy. The Bristcombes took my message to the village for me, for the two maids I hope to hire. They asked me for the afternoon off today."

"They often take a Sunday afternoon off," Jane confirmed.

"How have they been behaving?" deVigne inquired.

"Respectfully. They are *trying* to improve, I think. What are your feelings on my latest discovery, deVigne?"

"That makes it twenty-five hundred guineas. It is beginning to become serious."

"Yes, grand larceny is hardly a joking matter."

"Let us conduct the search. and see how much the total amounts to before we decide what to do about it. Any pixies in the orchard last night?" he asked next, in a spirit of civil inquiry only, as far as the widow could tell.

"As a matter of fact, there was one, which quite slipped my mind with the more important news," she answered offhandedly. She risked a close scrutiny of deVigne, but could read nothing except interest on his face.

"What happened?" he asked.

"I heard a noise, and took a look out. I could only see one man."

"What was he doing?" Lady Jane asked.

"Just snooping around, I believe. He didn't try to come in, at least," Delsie answered, feeling very warm at the memory of what had really happened.

"Ha. Maybe he left you another present. Have you taken a look around outside today?"

"No! I should have done so!"

"It's a nasty, miserable day," Jane consoled her. "No one else will have been there before you. You can have a look early tomorrow."

"I shall, certainly."

Sir Harold, who had been listening to all the talk, suddenly pushed himself to speech. "Andrew was up to some monkeyshines," he said, impatiently eyeing a book that lay on the table beside him. "Not a doubt of it. Where else would he have got ahold of twenty-five hundred guineas? A small fortune. And kept it around the house in cash too, instead of putting it in the bank like a Christian, or into the funds. A pity the fellow was ever let into the family."

"Good gracious!" Lady Jane shrieked, and turned pale around the edges of her rouge. "He wouldn't have invented a counterfeiting machine, would he? The man has turned coiner on us."

"The ones I saw were the real thing," deVigne assured her.

"Was certainly up to something crooked," Sir Harold insisted mulishly. "Running a gambling hell right under our very noses, likely as not."

"He wasn't well enough for that," deVigne explained. "And in any case, the amount of traffic entailed would not have escaped our notice these last three years."

"If it were that, he'd have lost his shirt," Jane said more bluntly. "Lost every penny he played on the market, and always lost at cards too, as far as I can remember. Never backed a winning horse in his life. Whatever it was, I wish we knew. Twenty-five hundred guineas. If it weren't actually illegal, we might continue with it. Well, Delsie, you are twenty-five hundred guineas to the good. What do you mean to do with the money?"

"Save it and make restitution when the case comes to court. I hope the judge will deal leniently with me if I can return most of the money."

Lady Jane sat mute at such innocent honesty as this. Sir Harold nodded his head in approval. "An excellent notion," he agreed. Then he gave in to temptation and picked up the book.

"I trust our cousin is funning," deVigne stated. "As I trust you were also joking about setting up a gig."

"I am not joking about either one."

"There is no way they can take Delsie to court, is there, Max?" Jane asked.

"Of course not, and there is no way Mrs Grayshott is setting herself up a gig either."

"I believe I can manage it on my new salary," she countered.

"With the sale of Andrew's cattle and stable equipment, you can do better than a gig."

"A carriage and team would be very expensive. The horses must be fed, you know, and *two* horses eating their heads off day after day will soon eat up my two hundred and fifty pounds. Then too, it requires a driver, whereas I think I could handle a gig myself, with a little practice."

"Why not make it a dog cart and have done with it?" deVigne asked angrily.

"My dear, I cannot think you would wish to appear in the village in a *gig*," Jane said, frowning. "If your own money is insufficient for a carriage, and nothing can be spared from Bobbie's portion, you would do better to just use my carriage or Max's when you wish to go out. I should be very happy to share mine, and you, Max, have several. One would always be free."

"It is understandable that Mrs Grayshott wants to set up her own, especially when *mine* are in the habit of arriving late to deliver her, but I should dislike excessively to see her set up a gig, like a —"

"Schoolmistress?" she asked with a pugnacious light in her eye.

"That was not what I meant to say."

"That's good, for I don't know of any schoolmistress fortunate enough to set herself up with a gig, and it is plenty good enough to suit *me*."

"But it is not, my dear," Jane contradicted baldly. "It is only useful on a fine day for a short jaunt. Why, even if you had your own gig, it would have done you no good today, in the rain. You need a proper covered carriage. It rains at least three times a week, and is too cold half the year to go anywhere in an open gig, as well as looking so very shabby. Really, I think it a waste of money."

"The sale of Andrew's effects will allow you to set yourself up a creditable carriage and team, and I shall be happy to undertake fodder for the team," deVigne said.

"There is a fairly good crop of hay in my own yard," Delsie said, as a jesting way of indicating her acquiescence in the matter, without actually saying so.

This was not good enough for Jane, who wished to have it settled. "Does this mean you have decided against the gig?" she asked.

"I shall reconsider it," she allowed. The objections raised had weighed heavily against the gig. Her wishes too were not averse to procuring a more dashing and prestigious means of conveyance.

"It would look so very odd to see you in a gig," Jane continued. "Bobbie too. For a child of the deVigne family to be transported in such a manner, like the Bristcombes."

"If it is not good enough for a deVigne, then I suppose I must not get it," Delsie said, becoming annoyed. "As far as that goes, Roberta bears the same name as myself, and I would not be ashamed to be seen in a gig."

"It is nothing to be ashamed of," deVigne allowed. "Louise once spent a summer jogging along the roads in a whiskey, and appeared to derive considerable pleasure from it too, but as Jane pointed out, it would be useless three quarters of the time, and it seems a shame to spend good money on a toy."

After this interlude, the afternoon passed quietly and agreeably. Roberta returned to the family circle, replacing Sir Harold, who slipped away to his library, without being missed in the least. Those remaining gathered around the grate to talk and play a few games of jackstraws to amuse the child (and Lady Jane, who

148

was an adept at this diversion). Neither did she consider a game of all fours beneath her dignity. With jackstraws, cards, and magazines, a quiet afternoon was enjoyed. Dinner was served earlier than usual because of Roberta's presence. She was allowed to eat with the adults for a treat. Similarly, the evening broke up early, at eight o'clock.

As they were driven home by deVigne, he said, "It is a little early to call it a night yet. May I prevail on your charity to invite me in for an hour, cousin? Harold tells me you are a fair hand at chess. If my conversation fails to hold your interest, I hope my skill at the game may be a compensation."

She had not been looking forward to a long night alone, and was pleased at the question. Her talks with deVigne more usually occurred in the midst of the family. She was happy at the prospect of becoming more intimately acquainted with him. "An excellent idea, but even poor conversation sounds more appealing to me than good chess."

"Thank you. I feel my conversation to be no worse than poor."

"I didn't mean that!"

"Can I conversate with you too?" Bobbie asked.

"No, ignoramus, you can study your grammar," her uncle replied blandly. "With two teachers, one hopes for some better progress than you are showing."

"How can I progress if you don't let me talk?" she asked artfully.

"I see you have progressed to sophistry already."

Mrs Grayshott entered the house with a high heart, looking forward to the visit. Her spirits plunged with the first words she heard from Bristcombe, who was there with lamps lit to admit them.

CHAPTER
TWELVE

"It wasn't my fault! I locked the place up before I left, tight as a drum," Bristcombe said.

"What has happened?" Mrs Grayshott demanded.

"We was broken in on while the place was empty."

"What, visited by burglars?" deVigne queried.

"Yes, milord, and it was no common burglar either, for the door was opened with a key. Must have been — there's no windows broken, and no sign of monkeying with the locks. He had a key, whoever he was. I locked up every door most particular before I left, knowing I'd be home early, before Mrs Bristcombe."

"It is all of a piece," Delsie said, and stepped into the hallway. "I suppose the vault has been broken into?"

"No, ma'am, it's only the master's bedroom as has been mauled about. We took a look all about as soon as we saw the back door standing ajar. The silver's never been touched, nor the china, nor nothing taken at all."

"We'd best go have a look," deVigne said, and headed to the staircase, with everyone, even including Roberta and Miss Milne, at his heels. They were not long in discovering the master bedroom to be a total shambles. The bed had been literally torn apart — the hangings on the floor, the canopy split open with a

151

knife, the mattress on the floor, also split wide open, with a quantity of goose feathers drifting in the breeze. Every drawer of every chest and the desk was upturned on the floor, the contents in a heap.

The entire company was speechless at such wanton vandalism, till Bristcombe pointed out to them that, despite the chaos, nothing here either had been removed. The silver-backed brushes left in place, and a little dish holding some rather fine shirt studs and tie pins and a gold watch not tampered with at all.

"He knew what he was after all right," deVigne said, with a meaningful look at Mrs Grayshott, who cautioned him to silence with a scowl.

"A pity," she said in a brisk tone. "I'll have one of the girls I'm hiring clean it up tomorrow. It is too late to tackle such a monstrous job tonight. I'll just lock the door and take the key with me."

Roberta was reluctant to leave the scene of so much amusement. She was busy kicking up feathers, and blowing them about. Miss Milne led her away, while Bristcombe returned to his kitchen, leaving Delsie and deVigne to go down to the saloon to discuss this new twist in private.

"He was after the money, of course," she said at once. I wonder who knew it was there. I don't put this a bit past the Bristcombes, to have done it themselves while the place was empty."

"I think not. They had the place to themselves half a week before you came here after Andrew's death. Why leave it so late?"

"He said the burglar had a key — an ex-servant, that sounds like."

"Samson," deVigne said at once. "Andrew's valet. I paid him off the day after Andrew's death. If anyone knew Andrew had money stashed in that room, it was he. No doubt he looked around before leaving, but the money was well hidden. You might not have thought to look on *top* of the canopy yourself, if you hadn't happened to notice it sagging. Interesting thing — he came to Andrew about three years ago, shortly after Louise's death. It was not long before, or perhaps after — in any case, around the time of Andrew's financial troubles, when he sold the place at Merton and tried to get control of Louise's money. Samson very likely had a key, or could have got one easily enough."

"He wouldn't know there was to be no one here on this particular afternoon. Unless he has been skulking about in the rain, spying on us," she pointed out. "What a pleasant thought! A villain standing at our doorway, with a key to the place in his pocket, to facilitate his entering any time he pleases, to slit our throats or set fire to us."

"That does not appear to have been his aim, cousin. He waited till the place was empty. Samson would know the Bristcombes often take a Sunday afternoon off, and could have learned with very little trouble, by simple induction, in fact, that you would eat out when your servants were to be away."

"We shall learn from the constable how he found out. I mean to report him."

"I'm afraid I can't let you do that," he answered, rubbing his chin and gazing into the fire.

"How do you plan to stop me?" she asked in a starchy voice.

He looked at her and smiled suddenly. "Wrong tack again. I ought to have urged you to dash off to Questnow at once in search of the constable, to insure your not reporting it. You forget, we have a little illicit business of our own going on here that we do not wish to call official attention to. Only think how embarrassing if it should come out that the valet — I assume our culprit must be Samson — tells he was looking for a fortune got by illegal means by your husband."

"He's your brother-in-law! Don't make it sound as though *I* am so closely mixed up in it. I suppose it *might* come out what he was after, but I don't mean to stay on here in a house where burglars are free to come and go as they please."

"You are wishing yourself safely back in Miss Frisk's garret, I collect? Don't you think it would be better to change the locks, and take your chances?"

Her bosom swelled in indignation. "It has been clear from the outset that *you* place no store in my safety or comfort, or you would never have made me marry this villain of an Andrew in the first place. But I should think you would show some concern for your own niece!"

"I am concerned for the safety and comfort of you both. If I thought there were the least real danger, you may be sure I would not permit you to stay on here."

154

"*Permit* me? I shall stay if I want to!"

"Oh, very well, then, stay, but I *do* think you ought to get the locks changed."

"Oh!" She stamped her foot in vexation at this subtle trap.

"You should really try to control your temper, ma'am. It cannot be good for your heart for you to be so easily vexed. Shall I send a man from the Hall to attend to the locks? I have an excellent chap who does that sort of repair work for myself and the Dower House."

"Very well," she sighed in resignation. "I have no doubt that when Roberta and myself are lying on a cold slab, your repairman will also construct a superb set of coffins for us. I would like my daughter's to be painted white. A plain pine box will do for myself."

"It would be more fitting to paint it black, as a token of your widowhood," he suggested piously.

"You would choose a royal purple for yourself, I suppose?"

"I am rather fond of mahogany, varnished. Bear it in mind when I am being laid to rest."

"Your sort lives forever," she said, arising in agitation to stalk about the room. "There is one good thing anyway — I got the money before Samson got to it."

"Possession of the stolen goods is considered an advantage now, is it?" he asked, following her perambulations with his eyes.

"I see no advantage in letting another crook have it. What happened to honor among thieves, I wonder?" Suddenly she stopped walking and returned to the sofa.

"DeVigne, I have just had an idea! The man outside last night — it was Samson, trying to get in and go over Andrew's room while we were all asleep. How fortunate I prevented it."

"I am curious to hear more about last night. I had the idea you did not tell the whole. How did you *prevent* his entering, when you did no more than peer out a window?"

She felt a flush suffuse her face, and looked quickly away. "Actually I — I went to the door — opened it. That's all."

"Why do you find that a matter for blushing?" he pressed on, observing her with a peculiar, knowing smile. "Come, tell me the whole. You went out, didn't you, when I most particularly cautioned you not to?"

"I took a step outside," she admitted.

"Foolhardy in the extreme. Don't stop now. You stepped outside, and . . ."

"Well, if you must know, he kissed me."

"How did you enjoy being kissed by a larcenous valet?" he inquired politely. No anger, no *concern* at her danger!

"It was not quite so bad as I had thought! There, now I hope you are satisfied."

"If *you* are, I have not a word to say against it."

She sniffed, and changed the subject at once. "I mean to ransack this place from attic to kitchen tomorrow, and I hope you will go through the cellars, as you *promised* you would do today."

"I hadn't realized it was a vow. No Bible was brought forth for me to lay my hand on. Come now, confess you are only angry because you have a devil of a job of cleaning up on your hands. Your life was never in any danger whatsoever, and the intruder did not get the money, so where is the harm? Why, you even got a kiss out of it! I will have the locks changed tomorrow, and you will not be bothered by Samson again."

"Next you will be telling me I am fortunate to have been burgled at all."

"A little excitement and adventure are the very things to distract your mind from this melancholy that seems constitutional with you," he returned reasonably.

"I cannot think burglary is the diversion a doctor would recommend."

"Very true, but there are so few diversions one can recommend to a widow without offending the proprieties. I daresay even a hand of cards on the Sabbath is not quite the thing. Shall we settle for my poor conversation after all?"

"No, I mean to begin the search tonight, but I shan't inconvenience you by asking your help." She arose and began peering under chairs, sofas, tables, and into vases for the canvas bags. After regarding her in amusement for some moments, deVigne shrugged his shoulders and joined in, investigating such unlikely spots as under lace doilies, candle holders, and in the coal scuttle.

"It is not dust and dirt we are looking for, but bags of gold," she pointed out.

There were few places of concealment in the saloon, and they were soon searched, after which they went to the dining room for a similar treasure hunt. Nothing of the least interest was discovered. They settled for conversation, enriched in the gentleman's case by a glass of brandy. Before taking his leave, he reminded her to lock the door.

"Much good it will do me!"

"True, but you would look a fool if you were robbed and had to admit you'd left your doors standing on the latch."

"I shall have the great satisfaction in the morning, when I find the study vault standing open and the money gone, of knowing I did my poor best."

"Put the money in the bank. It is foolish to leave temptation unguarded. I should have thought you learned that lesson last night, with Mr Samson in the garden."

CHAPTER
THIRTEEN

The widow passed a night undisturbed by any actual occurrence of a physical nature, but somewhat ruffled by the awareness of a burglar possessing a key, bent on breaking into her house. She expected to see her two ex-students bright and early in the morning, for she had asked in her note that they come at eight-thirty. At nine-thirty, there was still no sign of them, and at ten o'clock two squares of folded paper were given to her hand by Mrs, Bristcombe, just as deVigne came to the door with a man to change the locks. She opened them in his presence. She was shocked and dismayed at the two identical messages.

"My girls are not coming to me!" she exclaimed, frowning.

"Neither of them has accepted? That is strange, with work in such short supply in the village," he replied.

"I made sure I was doing them a favor. Their families are not well off, and I offered them fifty pounds each, but only see what they have to say: 'Under the circumstances, my parents do not feel they can allow me to come.' Word for word — they have worked this answer out together. What can it mean? It must refer to Mr Grayshott, but it is well known by now that he is dead. Is it that they object to working for *me*, their former teacher? Is that the feeling in the village, that I am not fit to be mistress of this establishment?" she asked her caller.

"Certainly not. Whatever it may mean, it cannot be *that*. Is there any use making the offer to a different set of girls? You must know many from your work."

"No, these two were the likeliest — good, reliable girls, with whom I got on particularly well. They liked me, admired me. If they refuse, no one else will accept," she told him, defeated. She was a little angry as well, for while they had refused *her*, she had an inkling that if the offer had come from deVigne, it would have been accepted fast enough.

"It is a pity, but I can spare you a couple for the time being. I'll have my housekeeper send down two. Come, don't despair, cousin. I'll speak to Mrs Forrester as soon as I get back to the Hall. I'll go to the cellars now, and you continue with the search abovestairs. We've done this floor. It will be easier for you to examine the spare bedrooms without a couple of servants at your elbow for instructions every ten minutes. It is always so the first day."

She accepted this small crumb of good from her disappointment, and went to check the spare bedrooms and later the attic, without finding a thing but dust, dirt, and one bent penny. DeVigne, returning to the saloon an hour later, with cobwebs clinging to his head and shoulders of his jacket, had the same non-news to impart. No canvas bags were found in the cellars.

"I was happy to see the state of the cellars, though," he continued. "A vast deal of good wine set by, and two whole hogsheads of brandy untapped."

"The brandy was to be your payment for the search," she reminded him. "Only fancy his having such a quantity of it — two hogsheads."

"I am well paid for my hour's work, but you are not completely unrewarded either. You will no longer be reduced to wrinkling your nose in distaste while I sip brandy. There are shelves of excellent claret and Bordeaux wine there, and a couple of cases of sherry. I took the liberty of bringing up some sherry for you. Bristcombe is cleaning a bottle now."

In a few moments, Bristcombe brought in the sherry, and the widow tasted it, proclaiming, on very limited experience, that it was unexceptionable.

"So it seems we have discovered the last of the bags of gold," deVigne said, settling back on the settee. "Only twenty-five hundred guineas — hardly a sum to get excited over." Mrs Grayshott looked her disagreement with this speech. "I wonder where it came from."

"I hope I never find out," she replied with great feeling and proceeded to enumerate aloud various possible sources, each more criminal than the preceding.

"All that brandy he had below makes me wonder whether smuggling was not the source of the money," deVigne mentioned, when her imagination had petered out. "Living here on the ocean's doorstep, and with Andrew's marine connections from the shipyards, it would have been easy enough for him to arrange it. He might have financed the importing and not taken an actual hand in the shipping, for he was no sailor. He was certainly in touch with the smugglers. Besides the two full hogsheads, there is one empty."

"What a pair of dullards we are!" she agreed at once. "Of course that is what he was up to! Every circumstance points to it: his knowing the sailors hereabouts, our location, not half a mile from the ocean, his own propensity for brandy. It is clear as the nose on your face. The bags of guineas are the payment for the various shipments he had brought in. It is just as Sir Harold said — he was involved in an illegal business, and here am I, sitting with a cellarfull of smuggled brandy and a houseful of illegal money. This is the busiest season for it too — winter coming on, and no moon to speak of. They do the smuggling on moonless nights, do they not?"

"I believe so, to avoid the revenue men. It would account for the village girls not wanting to come to you, if this business is whispered of in the village."

"Certainly that is it! I chose girls from the most respectable families I could think of, the very ones who *would* object, for half the village is in on it, of course. Well, at least we know the worst now."

"We *know* nothing, though it seems a plausible conjecture," deVigne revised.

"And the pixies in the orchard!" Delsie shrieked, then covered her mouth with her fingers as she realized the loudness of her voice. She tiptoed to the door and closed it quietly before returning to the sofa, her eyes sparkling with excitement. "The noises I heard in the orchard — it must have been the smugglers bringing the brandy into the orchard. I heard a horse or horses, or more likely donkeys, and men speaking in low voices. They were hiding brandy in the orchard!"

"You checked the orchard the next morning, did you not? You found nothing amiss there."

"How can you say so? I found the bag of gold. The smugglers must leave Andrew's share of the profit there for him to pick up."

"Seems an odd place to leave it, but, as you found no brandy there, they cannot have been delivering it. They were removing it. It was stored nearby, hidden somewhere presumably."

"Well then, removing it instead of delivering. It must certainly have been smugglers in any case. I am convinced of it."

"You are convinced on very little evidence," deVigne suggested.

"Every detail points to it. The bags of money — so many of them and all in the same form — payment for the various shipments. The noises in the orchard, the girls not coming to me, the brandy in the cellar, Andrew's connection with the shipyards."

"I grant you it sounds likely, and I hope you may be right."

She stared. "You hope my husband was a smuggler? Thank you very much. It is an admirable addition to his other sterling qualities — his drunkenness, his insolvency, his dying within hours of my marrying him."

"Don't pretend you object to that last item!" he quizzed. "But I had a reason for hoping we have solved this mystery. If that was it, the business is finished. With Andrew dead, someone else will take it over, and you shan't be bothered again. You have heard the last of the pixies in the garden. The lot delivered the night you moved to the Cottage must have been the one in progress when he died. It would take a few days, I suppose, for a ship to go to France and return, and wait its chance to unload safely. The shipment was already begun, and it was completed the night you arrived. The bag of money you found in the orchard was Andrew's share of the profit."

"I won't keep money obtained in such a way."

"Devote it to your favorite charity — underpaid schoolteachers," he suggested.

"On the theory that charity begins at home, you are implying I ought to keep it?" He nodded his head. "I shan't keep a penny."

"I am less scrupulous. I intend to enjoy every drop of the illicit stuff you so kindly give me. Shall we have a look around the orchard and see if we can find where they have been hiding it? If we discover some sign, we can take it for confirmation that this web of suppositions we have been fabricating is true."

"A good idea. We'll look for more gold too."

"A waste of time, as you mean to give it away," he pointed out.

She got her pelisse and bonnet, and they went to investigate the orchard for a possible place of concealment. They found no further bags of gold, nor any spot that appeared suitable for hiding some considerable quantity of brandy. "They were surely not so brazen as to leave it sitting under the trees, in plain sight," Delsie said uncertainly.

"I cannot think so. The Cottage is too close to the road. They usually use a much better hiding place — an abandoned building, an old barn, or an excavation where some building has burned down — something that offers a good hiding place. They would never stand it in a field and leave it. The deliveries might be a few nights in the doing, and to leave it exposed to the naked eye — no. That cannot be it."

"Perhaps they took it through the orchard to the fields beyond," Delsie mentioned, casting her eyes thence.

"They better not! If that is the case, they have been using *my* land for their work." He walked through to the end of the orchard, where the rank grass was undisturbed. A wild, natural thicket had been allowed to spring up at the point that separated deVigne's land from that set off for Louise and Andrew when the Cottage had been built, and there was no break in it. The unmolested state of the vegetation was proof that no regular traffic had come this way. Delsie followed after him. They exchanged a look that required no words.

"We *can't* be wrong," Delsie stated firmly as they retraced their steps to the orchard. "I am sure they bring the brandy here, to this orchard. But then what do they do with it? There are plenty of signs of traffic here, in the orchard, you see. The grass is all trampled down."

"You've been here a few times yourself, and I saw Bristcombe in here the other day as well, the day we went shopping in Questnow."

"The day I found the first bag of gold! He was out looking for it. It was only Bobbie's waking me so early that morning that led me to it before him. Bristcombe and I did not hold a dance in the orchard, however, and it would take heavy traffic to account for this degree of wear on the grass. It was smugglers and donkeys that did it."

They both looked around at the thirty trees, two of which were noticeably smaller than others. "Mrs Bristcombe told Bobbie these two are the pixie trees," Delsie said, pointing to the runted ones. "As the pixies are smugglers, these two trees must have something to do with it. She said they were worth more than all the others put together."

"That rather looks as though your housekeeper and non-butler are in on it."

"It doesn't surprise me in the least. I knew them for a pair of renegades the minute I set foot in the house. And the old she-devil so kindly making up the *guest* room for me on the far side of the house, away from the orchard."

"Calling you 'miss' into the bargain," he reminded her with a quizzing look. "Thoughtful of her; she didn't want your rest disturbed."

"I begin to wonder if you aren't in league with them. Telling me I should not turn them off."

166

"Only suggesting! It cannot have escaped your notice I never *tell* you anything, since you informed me you like to run your own ship. And I would hardly be cadging Andrew's brandy from you if I had easy access to a cargo of my own."

"Yes, you would, to blow smoke in my eyes."

"You have a nasty, suspecting disposition, Mrs Grayshott," he informed her with a polite bow.

"I have need of it to deal with this position you have got me into."

"I am very sorry I forced you into marriage with a law-breaker against your will and better judgment, but really, the matter is finished now. Can't you try to forget it and settle into your new life with some small degree of pleasure?"

"There will be no pleasure till I have got this place cleaned up and have heard from Andrew's creditors how much money I owe them. They will be pounding at my door today, I expect, when that notice you inserted in the papers is printed. Should I get money from the bank to pay them, or give them cheques?"

"Cheques will do. There is no need for you to go into town. Do you know, cousin, I have made a strange observation with regard to your marriage," he said with a smile.

"If you have made only *one*, you cannot have given the matter much thought!" she answered tartly. "I dread to think the observations that are made in other quarters."

"One subtle observation, that I doubt has been remarked elsewhere. Since we have leapt, the last few days, to the unfounded conclusion your late husband was a criminal, you appear to have grown fonder of him."

"I hate the very mention of his name," she objected.

"I wonder then what accounts for your calling him 'Andrew' now, when he used invariably to be referred to as 'Mr Grayshott'."

"That doesn't mean anything. Merely it is easier to say one word than two, and everyone else in the family calls him Andrew, so I have slipped into the habit without realizing it."

"DeVigne is actually two words as well," he pointed out. "The family call me Max, yet I noticed you have not slipped into the habit of calling *me* Max."

She waited for him to suggest she do so, but as he did not, she merely agreed it was odd, and inquired when he would remove the incriminating barrels of brandy from the cellars, carefully adding the words "deVigne" in mid-sentence.

"I'll have the girls who are to help you sent down in a gig, and it can carry the brandy back to the Hall," he replied. "Shall I likewise remove the incriminating money from the vault, and put it in the bank?"

"If you would be so kind," she answered promptly, disliking to accept so many favors from him, but assuaging her conscience that if it weren't for him, she would not be in such a pickle.

The girls arrived before luncheon, the brandy was removed, and Mrs Grayshott got down at last to the job of cleaning up her home. One girl was assigned to the master bedroom to do what she could with the havoc

168

concealed behind that locked door, and the other was armed with beeswax, turpentine, and a quantity of cloths and brushes, to try to remove several years' accumulation of dirt from the heavy furnishings of the saloon and dining room. They were young, cheerful, hard-working girls. Already by late afternoon the downstairs was looking better, with the furniture beginning to emit a dull glow, and the musty odor of a closed house somewhat lightened by the domestic smell of cleaning products. Through the front window, Delsie saw her husband's carriages and horses being led out of the stable and up the lane to the Hall, and wondered how soon she might be expected to be in possession of her own carriage.

She wondered also, when she viewed her dining room, whether it might not be time for her to hold her first dinner party for the family. The only problem was to discover whether Mrs Bristcombe, with the help of the two girls, was capable of putting on a full meal. Her luncheons and breakfasts did not lead one to suspect much in the way of culinary skills, though Bobbie had mentioned having better fare at dinner. Oh, dear, and the kitchen a shambles! That must be attended to before she invited company.

Dinner that evening was held at the Hall, at which time deVigne told Mrs Grayshott that he had put her husband's horses and equipment up for auction. The agent had mentioned a possible nine hundred pounds for the whole, which would provide her with a decent carriage and team for her own use. "I shall attend the auction and try if I can find a suitable turnout for you, if you trust my judgment. It would be ineligible for a lady to attend the auction."

She agreed to this, specifying only that he must not spend a penny more than Andrew's carriage and horses brought.

"Did you have any debtors at your door this afternoon, cousin?" he asked next. The notice had appeared in the afternoon paper, informing creditors to apply to her for payment.

"No, not yet, there has hardly been time. By tomorrow they should begin coming. I shall stay home to be ready to receive them."

"Couldn't you do that, Max?" Jane asked. "It will be unpleasant for Delsie to have to deal with the local merchants."

He looked a question at her, but she firmly denied requiring help. This much, at least, she could do herself. "I have been dealing with them for years. They won't try to pull the wool over my eyes," she pointed out.

"I had thought you might have the dressmaker in tomorrow to get started on your and Bobbie's gowns," Jane mentioned. "I wanted to go to the Cottage and discuss it with you today, but my joints don't let me about as much as I would like in this cold, miserable weather. We shall arrange it very soon."

"I shall write Miss Pritchard in the village a note, asking her to come to me soon," Delsie said, every bit as eager as Lady Jane to see her new gowns made up.

Over dinner, they discussed the various circumstances that led them to believe Andrew had been smuggling.

"A scandal and a disgrace," Sir Harold decreed. "Just the very sort of thing he would have got himself into. His Uncle Clancy over in Merton is the same, only of course it is mainly silk *he* brings in. The ship he bought from Andrew was not large enough for brandy. I wonder it didn't occur to me sooner."

"Where did you hear this story, Harold?" his wife asked.

"Everyone says so," he answered comprehensively, for he had no idea where he had picked up this rumor, though he had a fellow scholar in Merton whom he saw once a week to discuss philosophy.

"Strange we never heard a whisper of it, if it is true," Jane objected. "How is it possible the servants haven't been running to us with the story? It must have been done with the greatest secrecy."

"The Cottage is in an ideal spot for it," deVigne pointed out. "Well set off from any other houses, and close to the beach. No one would have expected a gentleman of Andrew's background to lend himself to smuggling. With a really good place of concealment for the goods, he might have done it without too much trouble. He was at pains to be as unsociable as a bear. No one was encouraged to call, including ourselves. What stymies us is where he has been hiding it."

"Taking it right into his own cellars," Sir Harold said.

"That is taking more risk than was necessary. There would have been no possibility of avoiding the charge if he was really so foolish as that," deVigne pointed out. "I cannot believe he took it into his own house."

"The men I heard in the orchard did not come near the house itself," Delsie said. "If they were removing the last load, as deVigne thinks, they were removing it from the orchard. I would have heard the commotion if they had been bringing it up from the cellars — the doors opening and so on. This last lot, at least, wasn't in the house."

"Right in the cellar," Sir Harold persisted.

"No, Andrew was a scoundrel, but he wasn't a fool," deVigne objected.

"If he was smuggling for three years without anyone tumbling to it, he was sharp as a tack," Jane declared, with a hint of admiration.

"It was a dashed rackety thing to do, but as I pointed out to Mrs Grayshott, I almost hope that is the explanation for the bags of guineas, for at least it is over now," deVigne said. "With Andrew dead, there will be no more smuggling, and she won't be bothered with anyone in the orchard, or with unwanted bags of guineas."

"I hope you may be right," Delsie said. That night she again had a visit from the pixies.

CHAPTER
FOURTEEN

Mrs Grayshott left the Hall early that evening. She had a busy day to look forward to herself, with her house-cleaning and her creditors coming, but of more importance, Lady Jane was tired and wished an early night. Nine o'clock was an absurd hour to think of going to bed, but sitting alone in state in the saloon was not preferable. She would go to her room and read. When she passed Bobbie's room, the lights were not yet put out, so she entered for a talk.

"We have a pleasant job to do tomorrow," she began cheerfully. "We must go through pattern books and select designs for our new gowns, you and I."

"I've already choosed mine. It's got ribbons," Bobbie said happily.

Miss Milne was with her, preparing the child for bed, and she too joined in the conversation. "I've been telling Mrs Bristcombe for two months this child needs new clothes."

"It's early yet. Let us get my books and have a look at them now," Delsie suggested. "Bobbie can stay up half an hour later for one night."

The three girls enjoyed a pleasant perusal of the books. As Delsie arose to go to her own room, she heard the light patter of feet in the hallway. It was the two girls from the Hall, running down to the kitchen to make themselves a cup of cocoa before retiring.

"Would you care for one yourself, miss?" the elder, Nellie, asked with a respectful curtsy. Then her hand flew to her mouth. "I mean ma'am," she corrected herself hastily. No resentment arose at the error on this occasion. The manner of it was not studied, as Mrs Bristcombe's had been.

"I'd like some," Bobbie declared, while the older girls laughed at her transparent efforts to prolong her staying up. They were young enough themselves to sympathize with the desire, and though Mrs Grayshott felt no need for cocoa after a late dinner, Miss Milne accepted, to keep her charge company. When the maids came back up ten minutes later, they bore three cups, saying Mrs Bristcombe had insisted on one for Mrs Grayshott as well.

"It'll make you drowsy, ma'am," the elder added. Being two years older than her mistress, she felt this liberty not too forward.

"Perhaps you're right," the lady agreed, and took it. Roberta was inclined to dawdle, with her new mama still in the room, and as it was now becoming late, Delsie took her cup on to her own room, to allow the governess to get Bobbie tucked up in her bed.

It was just ten o'clock when Delsie sat down on her chaise longue — she no longer thought of it as Louise's room and possessions — to continue leafing through the fashion magazines. How luxurious it was to relax at one's ease, considering future indulgences. Her eyes

174

lingered long over the pages with ball gowns of bright hues, of riding habits and fancy peignoirs. She particularly envisioned herself in one gown of a soft mint green, an Empress-line gown, with lace panels inset beneath the high waist, and pretty dark-green ribbons looping up the hem in swatches, with more lace showing beneath. Next year I shall have that gown, she thought to herself, and sat musing over where she might be likely to wear it. She saw herself at deVigne's table, dressed in a style to honor it. She must have some jewel to wear around her neck with such an elegant gown. Even a small jewel was not beyond her means now, with careful husbanding of her monies. A small strand of pearls was her modest dream. They could be worn with any color. And a set of earrings, too, would add a touch of glamor she knew to be sadly lacking. In a happier frame of mind than she had been in since her wedding, she went to the dressing table and began pinning up her hair in a more intricate design than she normally wore. If I were rich, I would have a woman to do this for me, she thought, and found herself wondering whether the elder girl sent down from the Hall might not help with her toilette. She dipped into Louise's pots of cream, rouge, and powder, to experiment with these dashing items. The rouge was not required, and not easy to apply either, but after prolonged efforts, she had achieved a result not too unnatural-looking. How Mr Umpton would stare to see her painting her face, she laughed silently to herself.

Glancing at her watch, she noticed she had wasted an hour in this indulgence of vanity, and with a guilty thought to the morning, she prepared for bed. Her eye fell on the cocoa just as she was about to extinguish her candle. It was cold by this time, so she left it to be thrown out in the morning. As she snuggled into her blankets, her mind roved over her cozy future. Her house would soon be in order, she would have a carriage, new gowns, a stepdaughter to add meaning and pleasure to her existence. No real worry marred her reverie as she slipped into a sleep that promised to bring sweet dreams.

It was the sounds outside her window that woke her an hour later. She had been dreaming of herself at a ball, waltzing in the mint-green gown with Mr Umpton, who wore a painted face, and suddenly the orchard loomed onto the dance floor. Her half-roused state tried to work the external sounds into her dream, when she was suddenly sitting bolt upright in her bed. Awake now, she could not believe she wasn't still dreaming. Impossible the pixies were back! Andrew was dead; the smuggling was finished; yet those sounds of voices, of jiggling harnesses and the clop of animals' hooves, were clearly distinguishable. With a rush of anger she jumped out of bed and ran to the window. The caravan — there were at least *five mules!* — was entering the orchard. In the dim light of a new moon it was hard to see, but clearly the sides of the mules were disfigured with bulges — barrels of brandy. She peered hard to try to distinguish individuals — dark forms were visible, but no facial features. Then she saw one shape clearly different from the others — a large woman, wearing white. Mrs Bristcombe, still wearing

176

her white apron. She could not make a positive identification, but she was morally certain who that one person was.

Fear was forgotten in the first rash rush of anger. Her whole impulse was to run down to the orchard and order them away. But she had not lived most of her adult life in a seaside town without having heard tales of the behavior of smugglers, and her next thought was to bolt her door, jump into her bed, and pretend to be oblivious to the whole. In fact, she did this, but the racket continued with really very little effort at silence, till at length her fear lessened, and she began considering what she might do without endangering herself or the other innocent ones in the house. She got out of bed, put on her gown, unbolted her door, and tiptoed down to Miss Milne's room. Odd that Bobbie slept through the noise, she thought, but a glance into the room confirmed that the child was not awake. On to Miss Milne's room, one door down, She entered softly and shook the sleeping form of the governess. What a sound sleeper she is, Delsie thought, and jiggled her arm harder. She had awakened more easily the other night — the falling shovel had awakened her. She began calling her name. For a full minute she indulged in this fruitless task, till it was clear the girl was in no normal sleeping state, but was drugged. Who would have thought that nice Miss Milne took laudanum? It was impossible to rouse her. She wondered whether she had the courage to go above and try to awaken the girls from the Hall.

Then she thought again of Bobbie, sleeping like a top when she was a light sleeper. Was it possible she too was drugged? It was not long occurring to her what ailed them. It was the cocoa. They had all had it except herself, and Mrs Bristcombe had insisted she have some too, to make sure they all slept through this latest smuggling expedition. Furious, she stood panting, while the full impotence of her position washed over her. She was in a house with no one she could alert, and outside the walls a band of villainous lawbreakers were piling up barrels of contraband in the orchard. She returned quietly to her room, determined to observe their every movement and discover, if she could, where the hiding place was. Tomorrow at the crack of dawn she would send for deVigne and place the mess in his lap, where it belonged.

The mules were being led out of the orchard when she resumed her post at the window, no longer bearing their felonious burden. Their sides did not bulge now. The men followed them, and two forms, the white aproned one and another — the Bristcombes, of course — silently entered the house by the kitchen door. They hadn't had time to do anything but place the barrels in the orchard, she figured. They had the impudence to leave their smuggled goods standing in plain view in her orchard. Her wrath knew no bounds, but she was helpless till morning. She must remain immured in the house, with the incriminating evidence waiting to be discovered by a revenue man or honest citizen who chanced by. It was infamous, and in her mind it was not her late husband so much as her husband's brother-in-law who was held accountable for it.

Little sleep was possible in such a state of agitation as she had achieved, but in spite of this, she was awake at her old familiar hour of seven. She dashed immediately to the window. The trunks of the apple trees successfully concealed the barrels of brandy, but she knew they were there, a barrel ingeniously hidden behind each tree. Of that there was not a single doubt in her mind. She was still a little frightened to go alone, so went along to see if Bobbie or Miss Milne were up. The child slept, but the governess was dressed, just drawing a brush through her hair, while covering a yawn with the other hand.

"Oh, good morning, Mrs Grayshott," she said, jumping up at her mistress's entrance at this unaccustomed hour. Her hands flew to her head, as though to hold it on. "I have such a headache this morning," she said. "I don't know why I should have, for I slept like a top. But with the *worst* dreams. I thought I was being dragged by a horse. Isn't that absurd?"

"Not so absurd as you may think," the widow answered, and, carefully closing the door behind her, she went further into the room.

"What do you mean, ma'am?" the governess asked.

"There is something very odd going on here," Delsie replied.

"Yes, I know. It is something to do with the orchard, isn't it?"

"Have you heard something, Miss Milne?"

"Only rumors, ma'am. I don't get into Questnow much myself, but my cousin Betsy at the Dower House made an odd remark when I was there Sunday. I told her about what happened to you the night we saw the man in the garden. I told her about the noises that happen there from time to time as well, and she said — she thought maybe it was smugglers."

"I think so myself, but it has gone beyond smugglers in the orchard. Miss Milne, I think you were drugged last night."

The girl's eyes opened wider in fright. It was not necessary to ask whether she had administered any laudanum to herself. She was horrified. "How should it be possible?"

"How indeed? You will remember the cocoa you drank. Bobbie, as well, slept like a top through the most infernal racket."

"What about yourself, ma'am? You had cocoa too."

"No, I didn't drink it. I heard men in the orchard last night, and tried to rouse you. You were in a deep, drugged sleep. I watched from the window, and saw them bring a load of brandy into the orchard. I mean to go down this minute and see if I'm not right."

"People *do* say it's better not to meddle with the gentlemen," the girl suggested, reluctant to comply with the hint.

"Very well, then, I shall go alone. It is broad daylight. I don't suppose anything will happen to me."

"You daren't . . . I'll go with you," Miss Milne decided, snatching up a shawl.

180

They went silently along the hall, down the stairs, and out the front door, opening and closing it with caution to avoid alerting the Bristcombes. Quietly they hastened around the corner to the orchard, there to stare at each other in speechless amazement. There was no sign of a barrel, nor of any disturbance. "I *know* they were here. I saw them with my own eyes," Delsie declared in frustration. She performed the futile gesture of darting to the back of the orchard, to see the rank grass untouched, its dew undisturbed, not a blade trampled down. "They were here. I am not mad!" she insisted to the doubting governess, regarding her questioningly.

"I had terrible dreams myself last night," Miss Milne offered.

"Yes, because you were drugged," Delsie stated firmly, with no outward show of wavering, though she was beginning to wonder if she had suffered a nightmare. "There is no point standing here arguing. I'll speak to Mrs Bristcombe about it."

"Oh, Mrs Grayshott, I wouldn't!" Miss Milne warned.

"Am I to cower from my own housekeeper?" she answered indignantly.

"If you think she's one of them . . . the tales Betsy told me of the village . . ."

"Yes, including the tale that is rampant there about *me*! My own students afraid to come to me because of the stories. It can't go on. I'll have this out with Mrs Bristcombe."

But when the steely-eyed Mrs Bristcombe stood before her at breakfast, her nerve weakened. Not in front of the child, she excused her cowardice. I'll speak to her later. "Did you sleep well?" the housekeeper asked, with a sly look on her face.

The gall of the question was sufficient to renew her fortitude. "No, I did not, Mrs Bristcombe. Kind of you to ask. I slept very poorly, due to the disturbance in the orchard. I noticed from my window that you were present, and would like you to tell me what was going forward there."

"Me?" the woman asked, with an amused grin on her wide face. "I was tucked up in my bed at nine o'clock, Mrs Grayshott."

"Not quite at nine, I think. You were kind enough to insist on making me a cup of cocoa at nine-thirty, if you will recall."

"Oh, well, it may have been ten," was the saucy answer, with a look that said, "Make what you can of that, milady."

"Then again, it may have been two," the widow replied frostily. She was suddenly aware of her vulnerable position. She and Miss Milne, who sat looking very much like a frightened bunny, and a child, were alone in the house with the Bristcombes. This powerful pair, allied as they were with the criminal smugglers — who could know what they might do? To delay bringing the matter to a crisis, she said, "I shall speak to Lord deVigne about it." I should fire her now, she thought, but was afraid. Her insides were shaking like a blancmange. She *was* cowering before her own

182

housekeeper, as she had vowed she would not. But before the day was out, she would be rid of this woman and her husband.

"I'll just see if Mr Bristcombe knows what you're talking about," the housekeeper said. Her manner became more compliant at the mention of deVigne's name. They did not fear herself, a defenseless widow, but they were still not intrepid enough to take on the lord of the village.

Mrs Bristcombe left, and the others sat on, Mrs Grayshott sipping a cup of very inferior coffee, and wondering why she had put up with the insolent hag for so long as a single day. She had known the first morning she came that they could never rub along. Bobbie was listless this morning, heavy-eyed after her drugged sleep.

"I dreamed about Daddy last night," she said. "He put an engine in my bed, and made it dance. It was scary."

"Now, isn't that odd," Miss Milne mentioned, casting a significant look towards her mistress. "I had a word with Nellie and Olive, the maids from the Hall, and they had bad dreams too. The whole lot of us had bad dreams."

Because the whole lot of you were drugged, the widow's knowing nod replied. They exerted themselves to make some light conversation for the child's sake, but as soon as the meal was over, Mrs Grayshott saw them upstairs to the schoolroom to allow her to proceed with a plan. This business was too serious to brook more delay. She would call on Lord deVigne, and shamelessly ask him to fire the Bristcombes. She was afraid to do it herself.

The trip proved unnecessary. He was on his way to the village, and stopped by to see if he could perform any commission for Mrs Grayshott. He saw at a glance that she was full of news, as he stepped into the saloon. "More bags of gold?" he asked lightly.

"It has gone beyond a laughing matter," she rounded on him. She opened her full budget, ending with, "And the Bristcombes will be turned off this day, as they should have been done the day I arrived."

"Why didn't you do it?" he asked her.

"Because *you* told me to give them a chance!"

"They have had their chance, and now it is time to be rid of them. This cannot go on."

"I am surprised you agree with me. I made sure you would recommend I let them stay on, serving us all poisoned drinks."

"No, I am not so fond of them as that. Give them their leave, by all means," he answered.

"I shall," she replied, but hesitantly, with a little questioning look, hoping he would suggest doing it himself. He was always interfering; why did he not do so today, when she wanted it?

"If you're afraid, I'll do it for you." Every atom of her body wished to grab at the offer, but the wording of it made this impossible. "They are *my* servants; *I'll* dismiss them," she was forced to say. Just as she closed her lips, Bristcombe stepped into the room.

"I have been wanting to speak to you, Bristcombe," she said, thankful that at least deVigne was to be present at the firing. There would be no impudence from the servants with him present. She was secretly glad too that it was to the husband she was to deliver her message. The wife was more daunting even than her grouchy spouse.

"I just came in to say, ma'am, as how me and the missus will be leaving you for good. We've had an urgent call from the wife's mother over at Merton that we're needed. They want us right away. Today."

She looked her amazement, swallowed, and couldn't think of a word to say. Her relief, she felt, must be evident on her face.

"Excellent!" deVigne said. "We rather thought you might be leaving soon. It was what Mrs Grayshott wished to speak to you about."

"We figured Mrs Grayshott and the little girl could stay with Lady Jane for a couple of days, till she can get someone to replace us," Bristcombe said, continuing his discussion with deVigne.

"A very good idea," deVigne agreed calmly.

"That is not necessary," Mrs Grayshott objected.

"You will not be comfortable here with no housekeeper and no manservant about the place," deVigne said, with a meaningful glance, whose meaning evaded her.

The last thing she wanted was to give Bristcombe the idea he was indispensable. "I have your two girls from the Hall," she pointed out. "We shall stay on here, certainly."

"We'll decide that later," deVigne said, with a look at Bristcombe, who appeared to take a keen interest in the matter. "Thank you, Bristcombe. That will be all." The man executed a clumsy bow and left.

"As though I'll miss them in the least," Delsie scoffed.

Her visitor walked forward and closed the door, shaking his head at her in a negative way. She continued. "I'm happy to be rid of them so easily, and only regret I hadn't the pleasure of firing them. And for them to leave so abruptly too — no consideration, walking out without a moment's notice. Not that I want them to stay!"

"You mismanaged that very badly," deVigne said curtly when she had finished.

"The mismanagement was in letting them stay so long, and that was *your* fault."

"It is clear they want you out of here for a night to allow them to get the goods smuggled in last night. Best to go to Jane for a day or two till the business is finished. They may have intended carrying on with Andrew's operation, but now that you have tumbled to them, they are eager to leave. They want only to get that load of brandy out of here, and you must go to Jane to permit them to do so."

"I will do no such thing!" she replied promptly, rising to anger at his imperious manner.

"Use your head. You don't want to become entangled with a conscienceless band of smugglers. Let them get their stuff off your property, and that will be an end to it. Get your things together. I'll take you to Jane at once."

"I am not budging an inch. I mean to stay here and discover where they have been hiding it."

"That is nothing to us. So long as they get out and don't come back, you may count yourself fortunate."

"I never heard of such paltry cowardice in my life!"

"It would be foolhardy to do anything else. We have no quarrel with the smugglers. Half the villagers are in on it, and if you run afoul of them, you may imagine what unpleasant treatment you will get there."

"*I* am not the one who has been breaking the law. It is not for *me* to turn tail and run. *I* am in charge of this house, and I don't mean to be put out by the Bristcombes."

"You can well afford to be put out for two days. What do you think to accomplish by remaining? You can't arrest them by yourself, and to call in the revenue men, you know, is tantamount to declaring war on the whole smuggling community. Your life will be a hell. If you care nothing for that, you might at least give a thought to Roberta."

"I *am* thinking of her. They have some excellent hiding place here. Who is to say they won't revert to it later on, if we don't discover it and get rid of it? I *must* know where they have been putting it. I should think you would offer to help me, instead of siding with a band of smugglers."

"I will keep a careful watch and see where they have hidden the stuff, but let them get it off your property. That is all they want to do. Let them go their way. They do no real harm to anyone — it is not as though they were murderers. They molest no one so long as they are not interfered with. They are not considered criminals in the ordinary way. I personally have no grudge against them. Andrew was working with them — they have got caught unprepared, with no place to take the cargo but here. Best to let them go on with it. Get your things together now, and let the Bristcombes see you are leaving. They'll spread the word, and by tomorrow or the next day the thing will be over for good."

"That's what you said several days ago, that it was over for good. Since that time we have all been *poisoned*, however! They have the gall for anything. I won't try to *stop* them, but I won't run away either. I'll just spy and see where they have been hiding the barrels. It is nothing short of magic, deVigne, that they took a whole caravan of mules, each carrying two barrels, into the orchard, and it vanished."

"They won't come for it with you here."

"If they don't come for it, there is nothing to worry about," she replied reasonably.

"They'll find some way of being rid of you, and it won't be pleasant."

It had become a contest of wills. In her mind, she decided he was trying to bend her to do his bidding, and she was bound to stay if it killed her. "I am not leaving this house," she told him.

"You mean to expose my niece to this unnecessary danger, do you?" he asked sharply.

"Certainly not. You may take Roberta to Lady Jane, or take her yourself."

"I will take you both. Pack your bag. We're leaving," he commanded.

She inhaled a deep breath and threw back her shoulders for the challenge. "I have come to realize you are very much accustomed to having your own way. I have seen the villagers tugging their forelocks when you strut past. My own former docility in marrying your drunken, criminal brother-in-law against my will may have misled you into thinking I am equally biddable. It is not the case. *I* am in charge of this house. You are in no position of authority over me. Nor of my step-daughter either, for that matter. I could keep her here if I wished, but I do not wish it. You may take Roberta. I remain."

"I take leave to tell you, Mrs Grayshott, you are a stubborn fool. Will you be so kind as to tell Miss Milne to prepare Roberta for a few days' visit at the Hall? I shall require Miss Milne's presence as well, of course, to look after the child. You shan't have *her* this time if you run into a gentleman in the garden. The treatment of yourself will be different as well."

"Don't think to make me go by taking Miss Milne from me," she replied. Actually it was a severe blow to be losing the governess. She turned and went to deliver the message to Miss Milne. As she angrily stalked up the stairs, she considered his words. How did he know Miss Milne had been with her, in the garden? She had not told him. She had said practically nothing — as little as possible. Perhaps Miss Milne herself had mentioned it.

She asked the girl this question when she spoke to her. "Oh, no, ma'am. I never talk to him, only to say 'how do you do,' or to answer a question about Miss

Grayshott." The girl was busy throwing a few pieces of linen into a bag. She made no effort to conceal her relief at escaping the house. "And are you staying, then, ma'am?" she asked.

"Certainly I am." She had only a minute to consider that if deVigne knew Miss Milne had been with her in the garden, it was because he had been there himself. It was he who had grabbed her and kissed her. Whatever emotions this might have raised in a more peaceful mood, at the height of her anger it was seen as an impertinence and insult.

When she returned to the saloon, deVigne stood with one booted foot on the fender of the grate, in a state of angry concentration. "I hope Miss Milne has succeeded in changing your mind," he said.

"She is not so insolent as to try," was the unyielding answer. "While we are on the subject of Miss Milne, may I ask how you came to know she was in the garden with me the night I was attacked by a libertine? *I* did not tell you so, and she has just confirmed for me that *she* did not tell you herself."

His face was impassive, untouched by shame at being found out. "It was myself in the garden. I did it only to frighten you. I had already told you not to go out. It served you right. It was my hope it would prevent a repetition of such foolhardiness on your part in the future. Your present decision leads one to the inevitable conclusion you *enjoy* being attacked by libertines."

"Not by you! I never encountered such overweaning arrogance in my life. Anyone who doesn't do as you order is stubborn!"

190

"I suggest it for your own good. What do you think will happen to you if you are caught spying about the orchard, discovering the identity of the smugglers?"

"Whatever happens, I cannot believe it will prove so unpleasant as my last experience there. And I don't mean to be caught this time."

"You overestimate your abilities. *I* caught you. I shall let Jane persuade you."

"I shan't be joining Lady Jane for dinner this evening. Perhaps you will be kind enough to make my apologies, as I have no carriage to go and tell her myself."

"You will find it a long day, with no company but your own mulish —" He came to a halt.

"I expect to have a deal of company. You forget your brother-in-law's creditors will be descending on me today, dunning me for his year's unpaid bills."

"It will give a fine impression, for you to be seen answering your own door before half the village."

"They will expect no better from a smuggler's widow!" she retaliated.

"You are determined to make this affair as unsavory as possible, I see. This is sheer spite. You do it to show me what an untenable position I have put you in by this marriage. I confess quite frankly, ma'am, I think it was an error. Had I had the least idea what Andrew was up to, I would not have urged you to marry him, but there is no need to cast yourself on the mercy of a band of smugglers to bring the message home to me."

"That is not why I am doing it."

"Why then? There is no sane reason in the world for you to expose yourself so needlessly."

"You wouldn't understand. I object to being used by people. I object to the open sneers of the Bristcombes, to their audacity in using this house for a smugglers' den. I will not be told by them or any persons of such doubtful morality what I am to do."

"Especially *me*! Let me tell you, I am as finely tuned to the nuances of morality and moral turpitude as you, or anyone else. There is no outstanding virtue in stubbornness, however."

"I wonder that you embrace it so tenaciously." She examined him with her gray, assessing eyes, that hid all her uncertainty. She began to be assailed by doubts as to whether she were doing the sensible thing. She had relied heavily on Miss Milne's presence, and had secretly thought deVigne would insist on helping her too, but he was bent on depriving her of every jot of assistance. "I suppose you will take your two girls from the Hall back too?" she asked.

"I shan't cater to your whim for heroism by leaving you to stand alone against the tribe. Do you want a few of my footmen sent down for the night?"

"That won't be necessary," she answered with the utmost indifference, but hoping he would prevail against her.

"Very well. Do you know how to use a pistol?"

"No! I don't intend to *shoot* anyone."

"It will be well for you to have some protection, in case the smugglers decide to take advantage of a woman alone."

192

"I won't be alone. Your girls will be here with me," she pointed out, the eyes widening in fright.

"There is no saying their boyfriends aren't amongst the smugglers. If it comes to a showdown, I wouldn't count on the girls for much help."

"You're just trying to frighten me," she said, hoping he didn't realize how well he was succeeding.

"Not at all. I am merely trying to prepare you for what will in all probability happen."

She wavered in her mind, half wanting to give in, but disliking to act so cowardly. He spoke on, still in the frightening vein. "Andrew has several guns about the place. Get one and I'll load it for you and show you how to use it. Be careful you don't kill someone, with it lying about the place loaded."

She had suspected before that he was trying to scare her, and was now convinced of it. She shrugged her shoulders and answered facetiously, to conceal her fear. "I don't want a gun. You will remember, when I am done in, that we have decided on a black coffin for me."

He scowled at her, but before he could reply, Bobbie came hopping into the room. "Me and Miss Milne are going to the Hall, Mama," she said. "Aren't you coming with us?"

"Not today, dear. Another time. Mama is busy today."

"We're going to sleep there all night," Bobbie told her. "Won't you be afraid here all alone, with the Bristcombes gone?"

"I won't be all alone. Nell and Olive are here."

"What if the pixies come?" the child asked her.

"Your mama is not afraid of pixies," Max told her, with a seething look at the stepmama.

Miss Milne came downstairs with a small bag in her hands. The three who were leaving made their adieux and departed. Delsie had to use every drop of her self-control not to dash out the door after them.

CHAPTER
FIFTEEN

Delsie looked forward to the day, and of course the night, with utter dread, but decided the best cure was work. There was plenty of it to be done at the Cottage. She got the girls from the Hall together and went with them to the kitchen to see what dirt and confusion the Bristcombes had left behind them. It was worse than her gravest fears. The place was covered in several years' accumulation of grime — the sort that had to be scraped away. She was revolted to think her food and that of Roberta had been prepared in this room. They began with the cupboards, washing the walls and shelves and emptying every pot and bottle in the place, many of which were covered in green mold, holding some anomalous congealed mass of food whose original state was beyond imagining or detecting from the odor. The widow first took a supervisory role, but as the morning wore on and she was undisturbed by any creditors come to dun her, she rolled up her sleeves and joined the girls in the Herculean task of bringing order to her kitchen.

Finding their temporary mistress congenial, the girls did not hesitate to chatter and gossip together, and after an hour they were directing several friendly remarks to Mrs Grayshott as well. They began by a comparison to how the kitchens at the Hall were kept — all was above reproach, and almost above their most exalted praise from what the mistress could gather. The words "his lordship" were introduced freely, and though Delsie realized full well she ought not to gossip, she kept her ears open and allowed the servants to do so. The girls' conversation with herself was of an unexceptionable sort — about the Cottage, her plans for it, and also about the school. Nell had a brother there whose progress could be reported on.

"He doesn't like Mr Perkins half as much as he liked you," Nell told her, "though he says he's better than Mr Umpton."

At one o'clock, Delsie went to wash for lunch, a tray with cold meat and bread in the study, and as she was finishing this, her knocker sounded. Expecting a creditor, she put on her most dignified expression, which rapidly changed to a smile of infinite relief when it was Lady Jane who stood at the door.

"I'm a ninnyhammer!" the dame declared. "Knocking at your door, when I know perfectly well the Bristcombes have left. I ought to have just walked in. I am all agog to hear about it, my dear," she continued, stepping in. "DeVigne has been with me this hour and is in the boughs that you won't leave. When did they shab off on you?"

"This morning."

"Good riddance. I am happy to see the back of that slovenly pair. And where the deuce can they be hiding the brandy? Vanished, Max says. Bah — it cannot be invisible, and we must find it."

"You are welcome to try your hand, milady. I have been over the orchard and vicinity with a fine-tooth comb, and cannot find a trace of it. I even looked up in the branches to see if they were possibly hiding it up there, but they aren't."

"We'll be on the lookout when they come to take it away. Very proper of you to insist upon staying here, though you cannot stay alone, of course. I mean to come to bear you company, and bring a brace of good stout footmen with me."

These words were music to the widow's ears. Somehow, it seemed impossible that harm would come to her with Lady Jane standing imperiously at her side. She was also happy for moral support from such a worthy source. DeVigne could not think her the fool she was beginning to feel herself, when Lady Jane supported her.

The day she so dreaded in anticipation soon took on the merry glow of a party. Lady Jane hiked up her skirts and went over the orchard inch by inch, even sniffing the ground and declaring at intervals that she could *smell* the stuff, but demmed if she could see a trace of it. She refused to leave even to pack her bag for the night. She sent Nell over to the Dower House with instructions to have her woman pack her bag and come herself to add to the reinforcements. The footmen came, bearing ancient guns from Sir Harold's gun cupboard, antiques actually, but in working order. The meals served were in the nature of a snack, but were enjoyed heartily. As darkness settled in, the two ladies took up a seat in the saloon and had a blazing fire lit to dissipate the cold and gloom from that room. With a decanter of sherry between them and a dozen candles burning brightly, it seemed impossible that danger lurked anywhere nearby, and they both remained in high spirits.

"I am surprised that no creditors have come to pester me," Delsie mentioned. "Andrew cannot have drawn a single penny from the annual income, for it is still in the bank. I was sure he would have staggering bills throughout the village."

"He must have paid cash from his smuggling money," Jane opined. "So much the better for you. You'll have need of the whole of it to spruce this house up. New draperies are wanted in here, and Max tells me the place has been stripped of linen. That is the sort of low cunning I despise. One expects the servants to drink up the wine and run out the back door with a leg of mutton occasionally, but when they take to stripping the beds, it has gone too far. We'll count the silver tomorrow. Not that it will do any good. I have no idea what Louise had, and doubt if Max has either."

"Still, I'll take an inventory so that I can keep check from now on."

"A very good idea. And the knickknacks too. Louise had a nice collection of vases and ornamental pottery — statuettes and things. Just the sort of thing that is easily lifted and carried off without being missed. I wonder how soon we might expect the smugglers to come."

198

"They usually come late, about twelve-thirty or one."

"I'll never stay awake," Jane said, stifling a yawn. "Might be best if I have a nap and let you awaken me when they get here."

"I have had the room across the hall from mine made up for you."

"I wonder what Max is up to tonight. Lurking about the orchard somewhere, I expect. My, he was angry you didn't buckle under to him. The first time anyone has said no to him since he was old enough to shave."

"He was very angry," she agreed with some satisfaction.

"My dear, you have no need to tell me! Pacing the room like a caged lion. It is a sure sign he is furious. Max cannot sit still when he's mad. I gave him a good piece of my mind, gudgeon. 'If you had any gumption you'd be standing beside Delsie with a pistol in your hand, instead of trying to frighten the wits out of her with foolish stories of atrocities commited by the smugglers,' I told him. All nonsense, the lot of it. They are not at all vicious nowadays. They were used to be years ago. Captain Marjoram — you wouldn't remember him, I daresay. Led quite a rapacious crew, not above killing anyone who got in their way, but it is no such a thing now. A tap on the head is the worst you may expect and it is worth that to find out where the devil Andrew has been stashing the stuff. My cook's husband is in on it — Darby Gibbs — but not one word could I pry out of her. They have to keep it mum, of course. Only natural. Max thinks the reason no rumors of this business have reached us is that half our own servants are in on it. I expect he is quite right. He usually is. And it would be so very convenient for Andrew, to have recruited his team so close to home. I have done everything but compose a song in honor of the gentlemen to try to get one of my servants to confess the whole to me. No luck, however. It is well enough for servants to dabble a little in the business, but it was too bad of Andrew to involve himself. Well, he never was quite the thing."

"Do you really think deVigne will be on watch outside?" Delsie asked, finding this fact of more interest than the dame's views on smuggling.

"He is not the spineless creature his behavior in this case might lead you to believe. Certainly *he* won't miss out on the fun. He was only trying to bully you into leaving for your own safety. The men like to keep all the excitement to themselves, but we fooled them this time. Harold, now, he doesn't care a hoot for excitement. He gets his fun from his books. You'll never guess what he is doing tonight, while we have a visit from smugglers to look forward to. He is reading the letters of Pliny the Younger, whoever *that* may be. He sounds a goosecap like Harold. What must he do while Mount Vesuvius was erupting but sit in his garden reading a book. I daresay he didn't even bother looking up to see the lava pouring down on all those people across the bay. There is no accounting for human nature."

"Sir Harold is very bookish. Was he always so?"

"Forever. He was born with a book in his hands, as some are born with a silver spoon in their mouths. You must wonder I ever married him, or he me, for that matter. It was arranged, of course, as most marriages were in those days. It was arranged in the same way for my sister to marry Pierre. You recall I mentioned Max's father, Pierre? A very dictator. Had *he* been alive, Louise would have married where she was told."

"It might have saved a great deal of bother if her father had lived."

"Aye, so it might. They had their eye on a marquess for her. My own papa was an earl. But Louise was always headstrong and stubborn. With Pierre dead, she got the bit in her teeth and Max could not rule her. I have a *little* of the same stubbornness myself. Harold didn't fancy my coming here, but here I am, and here I mean to stay. I hope my staying works out as well as my marriage. These arranged affairs work out as well as the other in the long run. I have been happy with Harold. Well, content, which is what we usually mean when we say happy. He does not set his back up against most of the things I want to do, and when he does, I pay him no heed. A husband who can be ignored is great blessing, Delsie. Let the youngsters prate of love as they please. Look at where it dumped Louise and Bobbie."

Delsie cast a commiserating look on her unromantical friend. Jane was regarding her quizzically. The old lady's eyes held a light, making her aware that this was more than a mere philosophical discussion of marriages in general. "I could never be married to a dictator like that Pierre, and Max is similar, but not quite as bad. Still, if you were his wife instead of only his brother-in-law's widow, you'd be locked in a room at the Hall this night, doing as *he* said."

"Let us hope he finds a biddable wife for himself," Delsie answered, but her mind was elsewhere. *She is hinting me away from Max! Is it possible she thinks I want to marry him?* She felt a sudden spurt of dislike for kindly Lady Jane.

"Ah, well, there's the mischief in it. Those dictators want a girl with a strong backbone, so they'll have the pleasure of breaking her spirit. A milksop would not do for Max in the least. He'll go on pulling crows with me and you if he marries someone with no spirit. I mean to see that doesn't happen. I am too old to be forever at daggers drawn with him. Between the two of us, we'll find him a proper lady with the fortitude to stand up to him." The cunning eyes regarded Mrs Grayshott closely, observing the little stiffening of her spine, the sparkle of anger that entered her eyes.

"I have a certain Miss Haversham in my eye," she continued blandly. "I'll make you acquainted with her one of these days, and you can tell me what you think."

Delsie suddenly found herself taking an unaccountable disliking to the name Haversham, but her reply was, "I shall look forward to it, milady. I agree with you that *we* shall not be bothered with his overbearing ways. We must find him a full-time sparring partner."

The dame nodded her head in satisfaction. "I'm done in," was her next statement. "I'll amble on up to bed, but be sure to rouse me when you hear the fellows in the orchard. I don't want to miss out on the fun."

Delsie sat on alone, going over the conversation. She was not surprised to learn plans were afoot to find deVigne a wife. For several years this matter had been spoken of in the village as inevitable. She wondered that Lady Jane had undertaken to speak of it to her on this particular occasion. Had she taken the idea that she had set her cap at him? Going over her own behavior, she conceded it had been perhaps too free. She had slipped too easily into a sort of intimacy with deVigne. Naturally the family would dislike to see him make such an uneven match. Her lips curved in a soft smile as she considered the scene likely to ensue if anyone attempted to hint to the Dictator where he ought to look for a wife. She did not think Miss Haversham's chance for success very great if she counted on Lady Jane's persuasions to do the job for her.

As the hour grew later, and as she thought her rest might well be disturbed with company, she decided to retire. She went to have a last word with the footmen, who were stationed at the kitchen window, with all lights extinguished. They, were taking turns about, one resting while the other watched. At any sign of action, they were to use the Chinese gong in the dining room to arouse the ladies. They deemed the hour early enough to risk having a lamp lit while Mrs Grayshott made them coffee to help pass the time, before going up to her room.

Sleep was slow in coming, with the excitement of an invasion to look forward to. When the hands of the clock pointed to one, she had still not closed an eye. At that hour, she went to the window and stood looking into a motionless orchard for some fifteen minutes. This vigil tired her, and she went back to bed to sleep through an uninterrupted night.

"What a take-in," Lady Jane declared the next morning, disgruntled. "A night spent on a lumpy mattress in a strange room, all to no avail. There is no point in my hanging about here all day long. I'll go over to see how Harold does, and return to you for dinner this evening, but I shall leave the footmen, just in case. Those two are to be trusted completely. Dissenters, both of them. They will not take so much as a glass of small ale, let alone approve of brandy."

"I must be home in case creditors come. Perhaps Miss Milne will bring Bobbie to visit me. There can be no danger in the middle of the day."

"I'll send Harold over to entertain you later on. Just ask him what he thinks of Pliny, and that will set him off."

This sounded more tedious than being alone, but Delsie was too polite to request that Jane keep her boring husband at home, and said she would be happy to see him.

"Happier to see him go," was the knowing answer. Lady Jane managed to be content with very little, in her friend's view. Even a refractory husband would be better than a Harold.

Sir Harold did indeed call that same morning, confirming the opinion that he must have provided the lively Lady Jane an unsatisfactory companion all these years. As he found the lady of the house with an apron wrapped around her skirt, busily polishing her own windows, he did no more than sit for fifteen minutes watching her, and uttering a few comments on the invention of glass, the difference it had made to civilization, and how it had eventually been taxed, as might be expected.

Miss Milne did not bring Roberta, but at three deVigne dropped around, looking heavy-eyed, grouchy, and holding his head at an odd angle.

"You mean to continue with this nonsense?" he asked in a surly tone, taking up a post at the fireplace and declining a seat, to indicate that his call was a courtesy merely.

"Certainly I do," he was told by a good-natured widow, much easier in her mind since her action had the approval of Lady Jane

"It would serve you well if they came in force," he answered.

"I hope they may. We had a flat time of it yesterday, and Lady Jane assures me they are not at all a bad lot who bring in the brandy these days. She feels a tap on the head is the worst we have to look forward to."

"I might have known there would be no counting on her to act with propriety when it was necessary."

"I think it very bad of you to be picking on Lady Jane. She has Sir Harold to contend with, and that is enough for one woman."

"There is half the trouble! Harold has never controlled her as he ought."

"You forget she is of the same blood as yourself, quite set on *having her own way.*"

He glared belligerently at this speech, then began pacing the room. Delsie smiled to see him perform exactly as had been described. "How does my stepdaughter go on?" she asked, to divert him.

"Miss Milne has taken her over to the Dower House for luncheon. They worked upstairs in the nursery this morning."

"Which she could have done with perfect safety here. What is the matter with your neck? Have you got a crick in it?" He held it to the left.

"Yes, I must have slept with it at an odd angle last night."

She wondered on what log or rock he had rested it, and felt a qualm of compassion, for the weather was not kind in December. "You look tired. I don't think you can have slept well."

Pity was not desired. He stated in a flat voice that he had enjoyed an excellent night's repose, while he walked briskly from grate to window and back.

"It would be a result of all the exercise you get, pouncing around the room," she suggested lightly.

He sat on the edge of a chair. "I think you should go to the Dower House with Lady Jane tonight. It is hard on her, an older woman, being out of her bed. It is clear the smugglers don't intend to come while you are here. You are causing everyone a vast deal of bother with this cork-brained scheme."

"It is no such thing. Lady Jane enjoyed herself excessively. She agrees with me it would be very mean-spirited to let them go without finding where they have been hiding the brandy."

"We'll discover that all right!" He rose again from the chair and paced in the other direction across the room this time.

206

"It has already been arranged. Lady Jane comes to me again tonight. You waste your time, deVigne, trying to bring us round your thumb."

They were interrupted by a knocking at the front door. "My first creditor!" Mrs Grayshott exclaimed.

"I'll get it," deVigne said, heading to the door. When he came into the saloon, it was no creditor who accompanied him, but Andrew's uncle, Clancy Grayshott, known slightly to the widow from his having been presented to her at the time of Andrew's funeral. He resembled Andrew, but was older, an altogether bigger man, and less refined.

After a few common civilities, Clancy said, "Where is Bristcombe today?"

"The Bristcombes are no longer with me," Delsie answered. "Mrs Bristcombe's mother required them in Merton. They left yesterday."

His nod held no surprise, and she took the idea that Clancy Grayshott already knew this. As he lived in Merton himself, it would be odd if he did not know it. Certainly in Questnow all items of gossip were known in an hour. "Ah, then you are left short-handed, ma'am. Perhaps you will be inclined on that account to accept the offer I am come here to make you."

"What offer is that, Mr Grayshott?" she asked, suspicious.

"I am eager to have my great-niece come to me for a few days. I had expected the pleasure of being her guardian, as you may have heard, but, being deprived of that, I would ask you to bring her to visit my wife and myself at Merton till the weekend."

"I'm afraid it is impossible for us to go at the present time," she answered promptly. A visit to this man's home would be her last choice at any time. She was sure that on this point, at least, deVigne would agree with her. Her marriage had been arranged to keep Bobbie away from Clancy Grayshott, but she soon found herself to be in error. Really there was no accounting for the strange quirks deVigne took into his head.

"I see no harm in your taking Roberta to visit the Grayshotts for a few days, cousin," he said.

"She is not here," Delsie pointed out.

"She is only at the Hall," she was reminded.

"The Hall!" Clancy was immediately on his feet. "Roberta was left in Mrs Grayshott's care! It was her father's express wish that she not be under your guardianship, Lord deVigne."

"She is not under my guardianship, but only paying a short visit of two days to her uncle — myself — as she will soon be doing with you. Nothing forbids that."

"No, no! She *lives* here with me," Delsie explained hastily, yet she felt foolish. It must appear to Grayshott as though her marriage had been a ruse to get Roberta into the hands of deVigne.

Clancy appeared to accept her explanation. "If you can let her visit her maternal uncle, I see no reason why you cannot bring her to me. My wife is particularly eager to see her."

Delsie was not happy to see Roberta go off to Clancy Grayshott's home, yet his request seemed justified. She noticed too that he had not asked her to *send* Roberta, but *bring* her. This was hardly more pleasing, but it removed her one excuse to forbid the visit. Clearly he was not trying to get Bobbie away from her. No, he wanted a short visit from her, along with her step-mother.

"I shall take her to you one day, Mr Grayshott. I promise that, but this happens to be an impossible time for me to leave home."

"On the contrary, it is a perfect time," deVigne said. "You are without a housekeeper. I shall undertake to find you one during your absence. A few days in Merton will be a pleasant change for you, and when you return, you will find your house in order."

"I cannot leave now. There will be creditors, after the notice in the papers," she parried. His reason for wishing the visit was becoming clear to her. He wanted to get her out of the house to let the smugglers come and get their brandy. He would even send her and Roberta off to this horrid Clancy Grayshott to achieve his aim. She dug in her heels.

"I'll be happy to meet the creditors for you," he said.

"I had hoped to bring you and the child to my wife today," Clancy went on, unconvinced that he had failed, with the unexpected support from deVigne. "She has not had the pleasure of your acquaintance, ma'am, and you may imagine how eager she is to meet Andrew's wife."

"I could not possibly be ready to make the visit on such short notice," Delsie insisted.

"Tomorrow, then. I'll put up at the inn in Questnow for the night . . ."

"Stay at the Hall," deVigne invited. Delsie directed an incredulous stare at his speech. DeVigne loathed Clancy. To offer him the hospitality of the Hall was done only to make her position more difficult.

"I fail to see the great urgency for this visit," she said angrily. "I have promised to take Roberta to you in the near future, Mr Grayshott. In a week or two —"

"With winter coming on, it's best to do the thing before the roads become bad," Grayshott pressed on urgently.

"It is only early December. I cannot think we'll be snowbound within the next week. I'm sorry. I am very busy — everything in a mess here. It is impossible to leave at this time."

"My wife will be very disappointed," Grayshott said, peering at her to see how this new tack was working.

"I will be happy to receive her here at any time. I cannot leave at the present." The mulish set of her chin at last convinced him that his errand had failed.

"I'll tell her, then," he said, arising. DeVigne too arose, and together the two men left the Cottage. From the window, Delsie saw them stroll together down the walk and off towards the stable.

"That young lady has a mind of her own," Clancy said. "She'll come to grief, mark my words."

"She had better not," deVigne answered in a quietly menacing tone. "You understand my meaning, Clancy?"

"Can't say as I do," the man answered slyly.

210

"Let us cut line. We have discovered what is going on here, as no doubt Bristcombe told you."

"Bristcombe? I haven't seen him in a dog's age."

"Not since this morning, at any rate. How long will it take you to get the stuff out of the orchard?"

"You found that out too, did you?" He laughed. "Pity. Such an ingenious idea, I had hoped we might go on using it. Andrew was a drunken fool, but he had a way with mechanical contrivances, no denying."

"Is one night sufficient?"

"Oh, an hour is time enough, but not with a sharp-eyed busy-body looking over our shoulders. That wouldn't do at all. The gentlemen are right shy."

"She won't be here tomorrow night. Come any time after midnight."

"What have you in mind to do with her? She won't budge for *me*, and I fancy you've already tried your hand at leading her."

"I have a few tricks up my sleeve yet. Tomorrow night. And Clancy, this will be the *last time* the orchard is used."

"Aye, so it will. Pity. But I daresay I can arrange the same setup at my place, now I know how he did it."

"It shouldn't be too difficult," deVigne agreed, just as though he knew what they were talking about.

CHAPTER
SIXTEEN

DeVigne did not return to the Cottage after leaving with Grayshott, but at about four, Lady Jane came, bringing a picnic basket of comestibles and a ray of sunshine with her.

"What's new?" she asked merrily, throwing off her cape. "Did anything happen while I was away?"

"I had a visitor. Clancy Grayshott was here," Delsie replied.

"Has he been pestering you already?"

"Yes, he wanted me to take Bobbie to him at Merton for a few days."

"It is not to be thought of."

"I have promised him a visit — I felt obliged to when he discovered she is presently with deVigne."

"Max won't like that," she cautioned.

"DeVigne was here at the time, pacing about the room as you described to me."

"He came down off his high ropes, did he? I made sure he would be sulking and deprive you of his cheerful presence for a few days, to trim you into line."

"He cannot be so foolish as to think that would have any effect, but in fact he was in favor of the visit. He wanted me to go at once. When I declined the honor, he invited Clancy to stay the night at the Hall."

"What!" This startling intelligence brought Jane to indignation. "Glory to goodness, he's run mad! He and Clancy have been enemies forever. Why, he calls him a mushroom, and worse. I cannot believe he would let you go to Merton."

"Oh, yes, he quite tried to push me out the door. But it was only to get me out of the Cottage. He would send me to hell itself to have his own way. I wouldn't leave now if I were to receive an invitation to Carlton House to meet the Prince of Wales."

"That certainly would not be worth the trip, my dear. So what happened?"

"I refused to go today, but am promised for some future time. Clancy and deVigne left together, chatting as friendly as a couple of schoolmates. Cooking up some vile scheme between them, very likely."

"I've a good mind to nip up to the Hall and discover what is going on. Shall we send Nellie up to see how Bobbie is doing, and have her find out from the other servants?"

"That won't work. He would not have told the servants anything."

"Harold is coming over after dinner. He would not be put off, Delsie, but there is a decent library here, and he will not tax us unduly."

The remainder of the day and the evening were not exciting. Sir Harold's arrival after dinner did nothing to shorten the lagging hours. He had not seen Max, or heard any news from the Hall. Delsie missed her stepdaughter; she also missed deVigne and the family dinner. She and Lady Jane dined on cold fowl and cheese brought in the basket from the Dower House. They sat together embroidering after Sir Harold left. Mrs Grayshott was beginning a set of seat covers for her dining-room chairs, and Lady Jane was helping her.

They both retired early, sincerely hoping they would have company in the orchard, as this cramped style of life was not of a sort that could go on indefinitely. But the only sound heard from that direction the whole night long was an owl's hooting, followed by the terrorized shriek of some small nocturnal creature as he was picked up and carried away.

Early the next morning, deVigne came, carrying Bobbie and Miss Milne with him in his carriage. They arrived just as the ladies were having breakfast, and Max and Bobbie joined them at the table. Delsie fully expected that after refusing Clancy's offer, she would be more deeply than ever in deVigne's black books, that he would be pacing the floor and scowling at her, but he was in good spirits. She felt insensibly elated to see it. He complimented her on the progress she was making with her housecleaning, and also on the coffee.

"It was your Nellie who made the coffee," she confessed. "I must get busy and find myself a new housekeeper. Do you know of anyone who is available, either of you?"

"There's that Mrs Lampton whose husband was drowned out fishing last year," Jane mentioned. "She is looking for a position, I hear."

214

"She's rather old," Max said. "She would do for a couple of years. Shall I take you to see her, cousin?"

"Yes, please, if you are going to the village. I wonder if she will be more willing to come to me than my two ex-students were."

"It might be best to wait a few days," Max said, then looked rather conscious, as though he had said something he hadn't meant to.

"A few days will make no difference," Jane remarked.

"Ah, I have just remembered — the auction is this afternoon," Max said. "I hope to dispose of Andrew's phaeton and cattle and get a carriage for you, cousin. Have you anything special in mind?"

"I don't want anything very grand — and only a team, remember. I don't want to be feeding four horses."

"It is high time Bobbie had a pony as well. Do you ride, yourself?" deVigne asked Mrs Grayshott.

"No, I have never learned, and as to a pony for Bobbie, that can wait till spring. The weather is not good. There is no point feeding an extra animal all winter for nothing."

"You should have a mount," he persisted.

"Like the pony, it can wait till spring. I'm bound to take a dozen spills, and prefer softer falling than frozen ground."

"You don't fool me," deVigne said, smiling. "It is not the hard falling but the miserly resentment of providing feed that delays the purchase. Clutch-fisted. You'll be locking up the larder next, and hiding the keys. My girls will not take kindly to such stingy ways."

Jane looked closely from her nephew to Delsie at this speech. She said nothing, but her face wore a knowing expression.

Delsie replied, "It is not necessary for you to boast of the large way of going on at the Hall. Nellie and Olive have done your bragging for you. We are operating on a tighter budget here, however."

"How was the onslaught of creditors?" he asked. "The ad has been in the paper since Monday. The local merchants would have seen it and acted by now."

"There hasn't been a soul," she told him. "Not one. The hundred pounds from the grocer seems to be the only money owing. He must have been spending his smuggling money, as you suggested, Lady Jane. How shall I know how much to pay back?"

"That is carrying saintliness too far," Lady Jane opined. "I know you plan some charitable work with all those bags of gold you keep finding, but surely what Andrew spent before your time may be allowed to go by."

"What will you do with the twenty-five hundred?" deVigne inquired. For about half an hour they sat chatting in a friendly way, after which deVigne took his leave, promising he would let Mrs Grayshott know, after the auction, what he had purchased there for her.

"He's up to something," Jane advised, the minute they were left alone.

"Uncle Clancy was at the Hall yesterday," Bobbie said, trying for some attention.

The ladies exchanged a significant glance. "Did he stay overnight?" Mrs Grayshott asked.

"No, he didn't stay for dinner either. He just came specially to see me."

"Did he ask you to Merton as to visit him?" Lady Jane queried.

"No, I never visit him. Mama, can I go up and play with my dolls?"

"Miss Milne will want a lesson first, dear."

"I had an awful lot of lessons at Uncle Max's place," she began wheedling.

"Baggage!" Lady Jane laughed.

"That's good," her stepmother congratulated. "You want to grow up and be a smart young lady, don't you?"

"No, I want to be a smuggler, like Darby."

"What a minx it is," Lady Jane declared, simulating disapproval, while her eyes danced.

Miss Milne appeared at the door to remove her charge. Over her shoulder, Bobbie said. "I'll do reading, but I don't want any 'rithmetic."

"As you were saying" — Delsie reverted to a former topic — "deVigne seems in an unusually good mood today. Sat on his chair like a gentleman during the whole visit. Now, why did he have Clancy up to the Hall? I'll find out what that was about when he brings my carriage, after the auction."

"It is our having such a flat time of it that has got him back in spirits. He said the smugglers would not come while we are here, and he's right, as usual. I don't sleep well in this house, Delsie. I shall go back home tonight. I'll send the footmen back for the night to protect you. I can't desert poor old Harold forever. Why don't you come to me for dinner? Max and Harold must be missing us."

It was a strong temptation. Delsie toyed with the thought for some minutes, before deciding she would allow a few more nights before she gave up on the pixies. Jane returned to her own home, and Delsie began an inventory of the silver, china, and other valuables belonging to her stepdaughter. Halfway through the cupboards, the dressmaker arrived, in answer to her request, and her work was interrupted for the delightful task of being measured for gowns and discussing with the woman what patterns and materials to be used.

The time passed quickly. She had not thought it possible for deVigne to be back from the auction so quickly, when he came in just as the modiste was taking her leave. He led Mrs Grayshott to the front door, to see standing before her a very elegant black carriage and a shiny team of bays to draw it.

"Oh, it's beautiful!" she exclaimed, overwhelmed at so much luxury. "I must show Bobbie. Surely you didn't get this lovely outfit for nine hundred pounds?"

"We got a good price for Andrew's hunters. Macklsey from Merton was there and bid the price up. This whole rig-out will cost you very little more than nine hundred. A good bargain, I think." He looked to her for congratulations.

"That's a great deal of money, isn't it?" she asked, but her demur was only automatic. Her eyes were sparkling and her lips smiling with pleasure. When she climbed into her carriage and sat back against the blue

218

velvet squabs, she felt it was worth every penny of it. Not only Bobbie, but Miss Milne and the young servants from the Hall, ran out to admire this elegant addition to life at the Cottage. Just sitting inside was not enough. The family had to go for a drive for deVigne to demonstrate how well-sprung the coach was. A short run took them to the Dower House for Lady Jane and Harold to admire the acquisition. As it was close to teatime, the group took this repast together with Lady Jane.

When deVigne, Mrs Grayshott, and Bobbie reentered the new carriage for the return to the Cottage, Max said, "You'll have no excuse to be missing church now in rainy weather, cousin."

"Very true. And I must call on Miss Frisk as well, now that I am mobile. It is shocking to have stayed away so long."

"You've been in a state of siege," he reminded her.

This called to mind Clancy's visit at the Hall, and she asked him about it.

"I felt one of us ought to be civil to him after his driving from Merton to call. I only had him in for a drink before his long trek home."

"I thought you didn't like him."

"I don't. I confess I felt rather foolish to be caught red-handed, with my avaricious clutches on Bobbie."

"What's avaricious?" Bobbie asked.

"Greedy," her uncle explained.

"Are you greedy, Uncle Max?"

"Ask your mama. She's the schoolteacher."

"Is Uncle Max greedy, Mama?"

"No, my dear, your uncle is not without faults, but I do not find him greedy."

"What *do* you find him?" the child asked, occasioning a blush of embarrassment to come to the widow's cheeks.

"I find him to be *present*, and it is not nice to discuss a person when he is present."

"Aunt Jane says it's not nice to talk about people behind their backs. That means you can't *ever* talk about them," Bobbie pointed out.

"She has a point, you know," deVigne informed the widow, with a bland face. "For my part, I have no objection to a little discreet puffing up, even in my own presence."

"How smoothly the carriage took that large bump," was Delsie's reply.

They entered the Cottage together, where Bobbie was at last allowed to play with her dolls. "So Aunt Jane does not come to stay with you this evening?" deVigne confirmed. This had been mentioned over tea at the Dower House.

"No, I stay to face the horde alone."

"Why don't you go to her?" he said, but in a coaxing way, his dictatorial tone abandoned.

"Pray let us not start that old conversation again."

"Very well. I'll send down a couple of men to stay here."

"Lady Jane is sending some footmen over."

"Only two, she said. I'll send a couple more. Are you to dine all alone, then? I am assuming you let Bobbie and Miss Milne return with me."

"I am used to dining alone. Certainly, take them with you. I don't wish to put the child in any unnecessary danger."

"I don't see why you do it yourself. But you don't want to discuss that. Let us argue instead the matter of when you and Bobbie are to begin your riding lessons." This was debated inconclusively till it was time for him to leave. "I'll take the girls along to the Hall now, and come back to bear you company after dinner, if I may?"

"Don't feel it necessary. If you have nothing better to do, I should be happy for your company," she allowed.

"What should I have better to do than make you happy?" he asked with a gallant bow.

"I'd give a monkey to know what you're up to," was her undeceived reply. He laughed aloud.

"I see a schoolteacher does not come in the way of many meaningless compliments, which must explain your taking mine so ill."

"Very true. Our lot is not a happy one, but we are at least spared *meaningless* compliments."

"That was gauche of me. Your exception to it is well taken."

"I should have thought a noble bachelor would be more tactful when trying to bring a lady round his thumb, but perhaps he does not often have to exert himself to please a schoolmistress. And I *still* don't know what you are up to."

"You may be sure I am up to no good," he warned.

"I know that much!" she retorted, and went off to fetch Miss Milne and Roberta.

Evening was drawing on early now, with winter coming on. Already at six the shadows were being swallowed up by the encroaching darkness. The house seemed utterly silent, except for the ticking of the long-case clock which stood in a corner of the saloon. Delsie was restless. She first set a few stitches in her seat cover, then picked up a book and tried to read. This too was soon cast aside, and she sat looking into the changing pattern of the flames in the grate, wishing she were at the Dower House with Lady Jane, Sir Harold, and deVigne. This was foolishness, depriving herself of so much pleasure for the questionable privilege of spying on a bunch of smugglers. And if she were caught, of being hit on the head. Tomorrow she would go to Lady Jane and admit herself bested.

CHAPTER
SEVENTEEN

She was surprised at deVigne's early return to keep her company. She had not yet dined herself, and thought he must have made a hasty meal to be back within an hour. He was admitted by one of Lady Jane's footmen, playing butler till his services were required for more daring pursuits.

"I didn't expect you so early!" she exclaimed when he stepped in.

"Nor did I expect to see you totally unoccupied," he answered, noticing that she sat with her hands folded in her lap.

"Not *totally* unoccupied. I have been thinking."

"A wearying pastime," he commented, taking a seat beside her. "Am I to hear your deep thoughts, or are they a secret?"

"No, they're not a secret. I give up."

He looked perplexed. "So do I. Explain yourself, if you please."

"I have come to agree with you that the smugglers don't mean to return while I am here. I want to have the thing over and done with. I shall go to Lady Jane tomorrow night."

"Delsie!" He sounded quite angry, causing her to stare at him.

"What's the matter? I thought you would be pleased. You have tried hard enough to pry me out, taking away my child and her governess, scaring me out of my wits with talk of needing guns and smugglers taking advantage of me. Even trying to send me off to visit that horrid Clancy Grayshott. Now don't tell me you want me to stay!"

"Good God, no! Go to Jane tonight. Nothing would make me happier. I'll take you at once."

"No, I have decided to wait one more night. Three seems a good lucky number. I shall spend a third night here, then tomorrow night I'll leave, and let them bring in their donkeys and carry off the brandy. We shall never know where they've been hiding it, but it cannot be helped."

"If you only mean to give in, do it tonight. Step down off your high horse gracefully. It is only a little after seven-thirty. Plenty of time to go to Jane. They won't be retiring for ages yet. We'll have a chat or a game of cards . . ."

"We can do that here."

"It will be better there," he insisted.

"I'm sorry I am such boring company," she answered swiftly. "I *told* you there was no need for you to come."

"You know perfectly well that was not my meaning." He arose from his seat and took to walking to and fro, making her realize he was agitated.

"For goodness' sake, sit down," she said curtly. "You drive me insane with that pacing back and forth. I thought you would be happy to see you had beat me, but you must have an unqualified victory. I must not only do *what* you say, but *when* you say to do it. Well, my mind is made up. I shall leave tomorrow evening, and not a minute sooner, so you might as well sit down."

He sat, with a sigh that managed to convey both weariness and impatience. After a moment he straightened his shoulders and assumed a cheerful mood. "Shall we play cards?" he asked heartily.

"Very well. And as you are *trying* to be civil, I shall reward you with a glass of brandy."

"Only one glass? The night is young. Bring in the decanter," he suggested.

She brought the decanter in from the dining room, but carried only one glass with her. "You don't mean to join me in my dissipation?" he asked.

"Not in this dissipation, at any rate," she answered unthinkingly, pouring out a small portion.

"How interesting. Name your own. I am broad-minded."

She cast a repressive glance at this venture. "This tastes like a vile medicine. And I must caution you that when you have finished this bottle, there is no more."

"Surely you will have a glass of wine, at least. Don't make me drink alone."

"Here is Nellie with my dinner," she said, as the servant came to the doorway with a tray.

"Setting up city hours, are you? Our cards will have to wait."

While Mrs Grayshott had her dinner, they talked of housekeepers, carriages, and a likely charity for the bags of guineas now reposing in the bank at Questnow. DeVigne, she thought, had set out to amuse and charm her, and despite her liveliest suspicions as to his reason, he succeeded. When they had finished discussing the present, he began to ask about her past life, commenting on the odd fact that they had both lived here on the coast for years without meeting. He teased her that she must have gone a mile out of her way to avoid making his acquaintance, for he was sure he knew everyone else in the village, and could not imagine how he failed to scrape an acquaintance with his prettiest neighbor. "Not so wide-awake as Andrew, obviously," he said, with his eyes lingering on her flushing countenance.

"Very true, and not so fast either. Why, he proposed before he was inside my door two minutes!"

"And here I was afraid *I* was rushing things. But you were not a widow in those days," he pointed out.

"No, and you were never *quite* so shabby as your brother-in-law," she complimented grandly.

"Thank you," he said with a hard stare. "We have managed to converse for half an hour without coming to cuffs, and I refuse to take umbrage at that challenging statement. You have earned a glass of Andrew's excellent sherry, and I shall pamper you by running to fetch it."

"That is not at all necessary. There are both footmen and serving girls all over the place now. Just ring the bell."

"No, no, we don't want our private coze interrupted by servants," he answered, arising to go to the dining room himself. This excuse was sufficiently flattering to please her. As she sat alone smiling, she had no suspicion that deVigne's waiting on her had a more devious motive. From his pocket he took a vial of colorless liquid and poured a hefty dollop of it into her glass, added the sherry, and stirred it up.

The unsuspecting lady accepted it with gracious thanks a moment later and took a sip, detecting nothing odd in the taste, as she was not a habitual wine drinker. After one sip, she set the glass aside and took up her embroidery needle. "Do you like this design?" she asked her companion, passing him the pattern she used, an interwined bouquet of roses and greenery.

"Very nice, but I am of the opinion ladies waste their time and eyes on all this needlework, which is, after all, only to be sat on."

"It is to be admired *before* one sits, and after one arises, and at any odd time one passes through the dining room for any reason. It is too nice to sit on, though, isn't it?"

"A great deal too pretty. Why don't you frame it?"

"If Andrew were here, he would devise an excellent contraption allowing the seat of the chair to be taken up and hung on the wall between meals. He was very ingenious mechanically. So clever, the little doll he made for Bobbie, that really walks, though with a very odd gait, I must confess."

"Yes, he had an unusual talent in that line. The Cambridge men are better scientists, I think. I was at Oxford myself. You aren't drinking your wine, cousin."

She lifted the glass and took another sip. "Sir Harold, too, I take it, was an Oxford man?"

"Yes, Christ Church, about a million years ago. He plans to donate his library to the college when he passes on."

She stifled a yawn with her hand and blinked twice. "Goodness, it is only nine-thirty, and already I am beginning to feel sleepy."

"A sad comment on my company. May I help myself to another glass of brandy?"

"Certainly." She made to arise to get it herself, but he gestured her back. "Perhaps I should have . . ." She stopped and shook her head, to rouse her tired brain.

"Yes, you were saying?" he asked over his shoulder from the side table, where he stood filling his glass. He looked at her closely.

"I should have kept one of those barrels that were in the cellar. I shan't have any brandy to serve you once that decanter is empty."

"I shall provide myself from the generous quantity you gave me," he answered, coming back to his chair.

"It is very warm in here, is it not?" Even as she spoke her lids became so heavy she could scarcely keep them open. "I must move my chair back. I am too close to the fire." He helped her in this job, and she stumbled against him. "Sorry. I feel a trifle dizzy."

His hand was firm on her arm, steadying her. "Have another sip of your wine. It will clear your head." He handed the glass to her, but she was too unsteady to hold it. He tilted it to her lips. She took one swallow. He continued holding it, saying, "Have another. It will

228

— make you feel better." She drained the glass, hardly aware what she was doing now. He had to guide her into her chair. She sat with her head back against the rest and closed her eyes for a moment.

Suddenly the eyes flew open wide. Shaking herself, she lunged forward. For a moment she looked at him, saying nothing. Her senses reeled, but through the mists she began to realize this was not a sudden fit of fatigue that had come over her.

"You!" she said, in an accusing tone. "You drugged . . . the wine. Oh!" She fell back, unconscious, her head tumbling to one side.

He observed her silently for a moment, then shook her arm, "Delsie. Can you hear me?" She made no response, but only sunk deeper into her chair.

He turned and left the room to call his footmen to bring the carriage to the front door. He took up an afghan from the sofa, wrapped it around her sleeping form, and lifted her bodily from the chair, then walked quickly to the door and took her out and placed her in the waiting carriage.

"To the Hall," he said to his groom, climbed in beside her, and they were off. He supported her with an arm around her waist, smiling softly to himself in the darkness as they accomplished the short drive to the Hall, where she was transported into the house in his arms.

His housekeeper was waiting for him. That capable dame had provided the other servants with jobs below stairs. It was only she who accompanied him to the Rose Guest Suite, where Delsie was placed on a bed.

"How did everything go?" the woman asked.

"Fine. I'm afraid I rushed it a little. It is not yet ten o'clock, and I don't know how long the laudanum will last. We'd better lock her in, just in case."

"How much did you give her?"

"About ten drops. She is not accustomed to it. She was drowsy after a couple of sips. I could hardly get her to finish the drink."

"She'll be asleep for four or five hours. We'll turn the lock just in case. I'll stay nearby and come and check every half hour. Sooner if I hear any motion."

"She'll be all right." He rubbed his hands in a self-congratulatory way. "I'm darting back to the Cottage. I wouldn't want to miss the finale. I'll be here by the time Mrs Grayshott comes to. There will be fireworks, or I miss my bet. Is Bobbie asleep?"

"An hour ago."

"Good. Thank you, Mrs Forrester. You are an angel."

"Funny I don't feel like one," the woman answered, looking at the inert form on the bed.

"Better a sleeping draught than a broken skull," he replied, and left.

DeVigne went to his room, changed quickly into old dark clothes, then went to the stable and got his favorite mount saddled to ride back to the Cottage. Four footmen were impatiently awaiting his return, as were Nellie and Olive. The girls were sent back to the Hall, escorted by Lady Jane's footmen, and from the raillery and merriment going forth between them all, it was clear the proceedings were no surprise to any of them. This left only deVigne and his own two men at the Cottage. They stationed themselves in a semicircle around the edge of the orchard, on the far side from the building. DeVigne was determined that between the three of them, they would discover the secret hiding place of the brandy. His own interest centered on the two runted apple trees, but try as he might, he could think of no place of concealment anywhere near them.

It was fast approaching eleven o'clock as the three men settled into their various hiding places, eyes and ears alert for the first sight or sound of company. No thought of heroism or battle disturbed them. Their mission was only to remain out of sight and discover where the smugglers had secreted their goods. If the elder footman happened to recognize his brother-in-law as being of the "gentlemen," as he had strong hopes of doing, he would do no more than roast him the next time they met. DeVigne was similarly interested to see whether Clancy Grayshott took any active part in the goings-on. He knew now he was the manager, but doubted he would see him tonight.

An hour had not seemed, in anticipation, a long time to wait, but in the actual crouching posture chosen, it seemed very long indeed. At a quarter to twelve deVigne decided he would take a very quiet, short walk to stretch his legs and be back at his post before midnight. The land surrounding the Cottage was all his own, and he had no fear of running into the gentlemen there. They would come up from the road bordering the ocean and fronting the Cottage. He stalked through the spinney, making as little noise as possible. Then suddenly he came to a dead halt. There were soft footfalls hurrying past him, to the right. "They're using my land!" flashed through his head. A grim, determined expression settled on his features, as he turned to give chase.

CHAPTER
EIGHTEEN

Mrs Grayshott began to return to consciousness within hours of the drug's having been administered to her. That the window was ajar may have hurried her recovery, as she had taken only a fairly small dose. In any case, she sat up, rubbing her head and looking in confusion around at an elegant chamber she had never seen before in her life. Her head swam and she returned it to the pillow, still dazed. She gazed at the ceiling, wondering that anyone should have moving circles on his ceiling. Andrew must have done it, she thought to herself, but after a moment the wheeling circles ceased revolving, then disappeared entirely, and she was staring up at a wedding-cake ceiling, with plaster moldings in the shape of medallions. How nice, she thought, and closed her eyes.

Soon they were open again, and she was frowning. But where am I? she asked herself. My room has no molded ceiling. She sat bolt upright and looked around her in earnest now. The corners of the room were in darkness, with only one lamp by her bed to ease the darkness of midnight. She climbed out of bed, setting her hand on the carved post to steady her wobbly knees. Then to the door — such a high door — it was at least twice as high as herself. I am in a house of giants, she smiled, and felt as though she were also in a dream. She tried the door, but it held firm. Locked into a house of giants, she decided, and returned to sit on the bed, totally confused. She was too confused for anger or fear.

As she sat on a few moments, her mind began clearing, and she asked herself in some alarm where she could be. Surely I went to bed at home, at the Cottage. This seemed a long time ago, and she had difficulty remembering. I was having dinner on a tray, and deVigne was talking to me. Got me a glass of sherry. The sudden drowsiness, the urging on her of more wine came back to her. She was not long in deducing that the wine had been doctored. I am at the Hall. Where else would there be molded ceilings and doors ten feet high! Locked in, and it is all deVigne's doings. Her first impulse was to go to the door and rattle it till she summoned help. But he was perhaps out there, waiting. She went to the window and inhaled great gulps of fresh air to help clear her brain, which had still a sad tendency to reel around.

He has locked me into this room, while the smugglers take away the brandy. He has been determined from the outset to get me out of my house, and resorted in the end to kidnapping. He had been talking to Clancy, had even invited him to the Hall, and had insisted all along that the smugglers were no evil criminals, but only a merry band of traders. Why, she wouldn't be very much surprised if he were one of them himself. Why else should he put their interests before her own? He liked his smuggled brandy very well. Didn't mean to waste a drop of it. Her spirits revolted at being bested by him — and after she had offered to leave tomorrow night of her own free will. She glanced at her watch. It wanted ten minutes of midnight. DeVigne, she thought, was not here at the Hall. He was at the Cottage. As he had brought her here and locked her in, she doubted she would be allowed to leave if she summoned a servant. She looked out the mullioned window — it was a high two storeys above the ground, but with a hefty vine crawling up past her window. She threw the window door open wide and tugged at the vine. It seemed very strong, and well attached to the wall. But would it take her weight? From the window to the ground was a long way to fall. She pulled with two hands with all her might on the vine, and it didn't stir an inch.

Without another thought, she scrambled out the window, clinging desperately to the main branch of the vine, and started her descent. It was really miraculously easy. It was strong enough to take a full-grown man. Only a few leaves, sere and dry in this season, tore loose from her hands and fluttered silently to the ground to tell the tale of her passing. Within a minute her feet hit the soft earth around the foundation plantings. She realized then that she should have worn some protection from the cold. The wind was piercing, but she had not far to go.

Off like a shot down the road to the Cottage. She knew she could save time by cutting through the spinney, but was unsure of the way. Approaching the bottom of the private road that led into the post road, she felt she could find her way now through the thinning woods, and this route would offer some concealment too. She turned into the woods, picking her way stealthily, running from tree to tree. Reaching a clear space, she stopped, then decided to dart to the next group of trees, perhaps a hundred feet away. After catching her breath, she ran forward. She was suddenly aware of heavy footsteps behind her. With her heart in her throat, she ran faster, faster, but still her pursuer gained on her. She could not spare time to look over her shoulder, but knew it to be a man, a big man, and very likely a dangerous one, bent on killing her. She wished, futilely, that she were safely locked up in the room at the Hall. That she were back at Miss Frisk's rooming house, that she were anywhere but in a dark forest alone with a vicious smuggler.

DeVigne had not gone more than two paces before he realized he was being foolish. He had his full share of the Englishman's sense of property. He resented that his land was being used, criminally at that, by outsiders, but as this was the last trip for the smugglers, he decided to let them continue. He stopped and stepped behind a tree to let the man pass. When he discerned the outline of a skirt fly past him, he knew at once who he had to deal with. He did not know how she had escaped Mrs Forrester, but from her direction, he was not in the least doubt where she was heading. The time was approximately midnight. He gave chase immediately, wanting to call her name, but afraid of drawing attention to them. He assumed he could overtake her in a minute, but was surprised at her agility, and in those clinging skirts too. He ran on, pushing himself faster, till at last he reached her. She was about to enter the next growth of trees. Beyond them was the thicket into the orchard. Impossible to let her barge in there at this time. He lunged forward and got his arms around her waist, but in a poor grasp. She wrenched free and plunged forward again. His hand flew out, barely getting a hold on her skirt. She jerked to a stop, then toppled forward.

"Delsie, for God's sake . . ." she heard her pursuer say, and recognized the voice. Then the blackness came over her in great, floating waves.

DeVigne heard the hard thump as her head hit some obstacle in her path, and was aware at the same instant of the telltale sounds of approaching men and donkeys. Not a word did they utter, but the surreptitious tinkle of the harnesses and the soft clop of hooves revealed all. On the ground now he edged nearer to see if Delsie was badly hurt. She moaned, and he clamped a hand over her mouth. He was aware of strange sounds in the orchard beyond, but he did not dare to leave the unconscious woman for a moment to see what was going forth. She might come to in a moment and shout. He peered at her in the darkness to try to gauge her condition. It did not seem possible she could be badly hurt. Her face was pale in the wan moonlight, with a black smear on the forehead that he took for a strand of hair. Touching it lightly with his fingers, he felt the warm softness of blood.

"Oh my God!" he muttered to himself, bending closer. The blood was flowing freely down her temples into her hair. The mood of the night changed suddenly. It had been an adventure, a diversion in life's routine, a pleasure really, and a challenge to discover the ingenious hiding place Andrew had contrived for the brandy. All thoughts of brandy and hiding places were swept from his mind as he pulled out his handkerchief and bound it around her wound, with his fingers trembling. His chief thought now was to get her to a doctor as quickly as possible. Not even a horse or a carriage — his mount in the stable at the Cottage. He'd have to carry her to the Hall, and the Cottage was so much closer! She made no move. Torn with indecision, he slipped as quietly as possible to where his footman stood peering through the thicket into the orchard.

"Hicks, go at once to the Hall and bring my closed carriage down the lane. Mrs Grayshott is hurt. I'll carry her through the spinney and meet you there."

"They're doing it now!" Hicks objected. "Gor blimey, they're moving the trees!"

"Go!" deVigne said in a voice loud enough to alert one of the smugglers, who looked up sharply toward the thicket, but fortunately to the wrong end. With a muffled imprecation and a last look over his shoulder, Hicks sprinted off. Having lived at the Hall since he was ten, he spurned the road and took the shortcut through the woods.

DeVigne hastened quietly back to where Delsie still lay on the ground. He was relieved to see no blood showed through the bandage. He picked her up gently

238

in his arms and walked silently towards the lane to meet the carriage. She stirred once and said "Bobbie!" in a hysterical voice, trying to lift her head, then it fell back against his chest.

"She's all right. Bobbie's all right," he assured her, in a calming voice, as he quickened his steps. Of Mrs Grayshott's own condition he was less sure. He did not feel it could be fatal, but a blow on the head might engender some mental disorder, possibly even of a permanent nature. There was no point in blaming her. It was *his* fault. Trying to save her from something of this sort by removing her from the Cottage, he had hurt her himself. Remorse was added to his anguish. She was cold as ice. Why had she come out without a wrap? His quickened pace was of no use. He had to wait ten minutes for his carriage. Ten minutes that seemed an eternity, with the unconscious burden in his arms, not stirring, while his impatience mounted to alarm, and finally panic.

At last the wheels were heard coming down the drive, and while an openmouthed groom looked on, deVigne managed with some difficulty to get himself and Delsie into the carriage. From the door he directed, "Go down to the road and turn around. You'll never manage a turn here. The minute you get to the Hall, go for the doctor at once. Take a mount, it will be faster. Close the door now, and don't waste any time."

He held the insentient widow on his knee, her head resting against his chest as they were driven to the road and back to the Hall. He tried to rouse her, saying softly, urgently, "Delsie. Delsie, can you hear me?" once or twice, but no response came. He cradled her in his arms, laying his cheek against the top of her head, silently cursing himself and fate for this ill-timed occurrence.

Mrs Forrester had already discovered the escape, and was anxiously pacing the hallway when deVigne carried Mrs Grayshott in.

"I sent a boy out to tell you she'd got away," she said, "but I didn't know exactly where you were."

"He'll likely walk right into Clancy's boys and have his head cleaved open," he answered. "I told you *watch* her, Mrs Forrester. How did she get out?"

"It must have been by the window. Who ever would have thought she would — oh, my! She's hurt. Is it bad?"

"I don't know. Her color is not gone off too badly," he replied, examining her, relieved to see in the better light that she was not so pale as the darkness had indicated. "Get some hot water and bandages — brandy. In the study," he added, hurrying in that direction. "And a blanket. She's cold."

She was laid on a settee in the study. Mrs Forrester returned with water and bandages, and was promptly sent off again for basilicum powder, and to find a boy to light the grate, while deVigne untied his makeshift bandage and examined the wound. It did not appear deep to his unpracticed eye. The skin was open, but the blood had stopped flowing. Why did she remain so long unconscious? As he began dabbing at the drying blood with a cloth, Delsie opened her eyes. She looked at

240

deVigne, said "Oh, no!" in accents of deepest disgust, closed her eyes, and turned her head away.

"You know me?" he asked brusquely, fearing he hardly knew what. That her brain was disordered, or worse.

"Where's Bobbie?" she asked in a weak voice.

"In her bed."

"I shouldn't have left her —"

"Indeed you should not!" he answered, anger rapidly replacing fear as he saw her wits to be intact, but the anger was truly directed against himself.

"It was you — in the woods," she accused.

"Yes, yes. All my doing. Delsie, I'm damnably sorry."

She closed her eyes, and they remained closed till the doctor arrived not so much later. During the interval, deVigne first sat beside her, directing a few disconnected comments to her unresponding form, then pacing the room, still talking at random. The doctor's ministrations roused her thoroughly, especially when he probed her cut. She wailed in a loudish voice that grew no weaker when she noticed deVigne glancing worriedly over the doctor's shoulder. After some uncomfortable minutes, the doctor closed his bag and pronounced her safe, with only a probable headache, which was to be relieved by a sleeping draught.

"No!" she declared firmly.

"Mrs Grayshott has already had a — sedative," deVigne explained.

"The pupils are not dilated," the doctor pointed out. "That must have been some time ago. I recommend a few drops —"

"No!" she repeated, more firmly than before.

The poor doctor looked quite surprised at her lack of cooperation, and said that if she had the devil of a headache in the morning, she must not blame him.

"You may be sure I shan't blame *you*, Doctor!" she declared in a meaningful voice, looking over his head to him whom she did blame. DeVigne shook his head slightly, to indicate she should hold her peace till the doctor was gone.

He soon left, and with a wary look, deVigne came toward the settee. "That feel better?" he asked.

She sat up and glared at him. "No doubt you are concerned that I be perfectly *comfortable*, after drugging me and locking me up in your house, and hitting my head with a rock!"

"I did not! Hit your head I mean. I had to stop you from barging in on the smugglers. Delsie, what in God's name possessed you to —"

"Oh, no, *I* am not the one who has to explain the night's actions. *You* are the one who has broken half a dozen laws. I shouldn't be in the least surprised to hear that moving smuggled brandy was included in your crimes either."

"I wish you will lie down and relax," he essayed placatingly.

"I have been relaxed to the point of unconsciousness for several hours already this night. What time is it anyway?"

"It is one-fifteen. Why?"

"You must hurry and find out where they've hidden it! Oh, do rush, Max, or they'll be gone," she urged, forgetting to be angry with him in her eagerness, and forgetting as well her vow never to use his Christian name.

"They've been gone an hour. They were there when you — you fell."

"Was pushed!" she corrected.

"I didn't push you. I had to stop you from dashing into the orchard. They were coming then."

"And you there to meet them! It is no more than I expected. I daresay it is you who has been littering up the Cottage with bags of guineas."

He dismissed this charge with no more than a baleful stare, deeming it beneath contradicting. "If you hadn't . . . and how the deuce did you get out the window?" he demanded.

"I climbed down the vine."

"You didn't even wear a wrap. It will be a wonder if you haven't caught your death of cold."

"A mere wisp of pneumonia will be nothing after the rest of it." At last she could contain her curiosity no longer, and gave over being angry with him. "Do tell me where they have been hiding it."

"I don't know," he confessed shamefully.

"You *don't know!* You mean we are *never* to discover how they did it? Oh, if I were a man I'd shoot you."

"If you were not a foolish, stubborn, headstrong woman, we *would* know."

"This beats all the rest! For you to be calling me stubborn after the way you have persisted in having your own way throughout this entire affair. Making me marry Andrew, making me leave the Cottage instead of helping me, and *then* not to discover the hiding place. Talk about *foolish!*" She stopped, too overcome to continue.

He looked a little shamefaced at these charges, and urged her once more to lie down and be calm. "We'll know the secret of the hiding place by morning. I left a footman there to watch and discover how it is done. He hasn't returned yet, but —"

"And likely never will!"

"There is no danger. Watling can handle himself. They were just beginning whatever it is they do, when you got hurt. Hicks said something — but I must have heard him wrong, in my anxiety. I thought he said they were moving the trees."

A tinkle of laughter rang out. "He thinks he is playing Macbeth, with Birnam Wood coming to Dunsinane. I doubt if even Andrew could contrive that. And the *trees* were *not* men in disguise. I hope I know a tree when I see it, and a man."

"I am happy to see your spirits recovering. When you take to bragging, I know you must feel better."

She was beginning to feel worse from the exertion of talking, however, and sank back on the pillows.

"It is time you were in bed," he said. "I'll call Mrs Forrester. Is it safe to put you back in the Rose Suite? Now that they are gone, you won't go clambering down the vine again, I trust. You are not here under compulsion now. If you wish to return to the Cottage, pray tell me, and I shall take you in the carriage. The servants have all left, incidentally," he added.

"I'll stay here," she answered with indifference.

244

She tried to walk, with the help of Mrs Forrester and deVigne, but after a few unsteady steps, he lifted her into his arms, saying impatiently that he didn't have all night to show her to her room. She was asleep before Mrs Forrester extinguished the lamp and closed the door.

CHAPTER
NINETEEN

With a heavy gray sky and her curtains drawn, Delsie's room remained dark till late the next morning. It was ten-thirty before she was up and dressed, and eleven before she had breakfasted. DeVigne was not in evidence, and at such a late hour, Bobbie was in the nursery having her lesson with Miss Milne. Queries of the servant giving her breakfast revealed only that his lordship was not in, which angered the widow unreasonably. Before she walked home in high dudgeon, he came in at the door, obviously excited.

"Good morning, ma'am. I hope you slept well," he said cheerfully, regarding the plaster Mrs Forrester had replaced, for she had no opinion of a doctor who covered up half a lady's forehead for a tiny scratch.

"Why should I not, with half a bottle of laudanum inside me?" was her uncivil reply.

"Good, then it is time to go to the orchard."

"Have you been there already? Do tell me all about it," she pleaded.

"I have just returned this minute. The thing almost defies description. It will be easier to show you how it operates."

She forgot her resentment in the exciting prospect of seeing her trees move about, and dashed to the door before him.

"You will want a coat," he pointed out.

"I didn't bring one with me."

He sent a servant for one of his driving coats, and with a very long, many-caped drab coat thrown over her gown, she was ready to go. "Oh, we must take Bobbie with us," she remembered, just at the door, causing a further delay. She remarked that there were several footmen accompanying them, standing up behind the carriage, and inquired the reason for this. "I haven't seen such an entourage since the first day you came to see me at the school," she roasted.

"I have been wondering when you would find an opportunity to throw that in my face. The trees do not move under their own steam," he said mysteriously.

Her hardest questioning revealed no more than this meager fact. Before long they were all, including the footmen, gathered around the two runted trees in the orchard, where chains and ropes lay on the ground.

"It was Watling who actually saw the thing being done, and he will direct the men," deVigne explained.

A lanky, lantern-jawed individual in livery stepped forward with great importance and picked up the end of a chain. "Take an end there, Hicks," he commanded, as though he had been issuing orders all his life. Two men were ordered into position at either end of the long chain, which was wound around one of the small trees. The men then walked to a position about six feet behind the tree, and Watling gave the order to "heave."

As if by magic, the tree tipped up out of the earth and was soon lying on its side. Its root system was seen to be encased in a large wooden-frame box filled with earth. Under the tree there was a stone-lined cavity large enough to hold several barrels of brandy, with a stone lip at the top to prevent the box holding the root from falling into the cavity.

"*Voilà*," deVigne said to Mrs Grayshott, who stood dumbfounded at this show.

"How? But this is *impossible* . . . ." she began.

"You underestimate your late husband. The other small tree moves on the same principle. Watling tells me both trees were lifted last night. Their being boxed in wouldn't allow the roots to spread, which accounts for their being smaller than the others in the orchard. A very neat engineering feat, I must confess."

"How was it possible for Andrew to have had this done without anyone knowing about it?" she asked.

"It is in a well-concealed spot — the other trees afford a good curtain. He did tell Jane at one time that two of his trees died and he was replacing them. It must have been done then. It wouldn't take much work, once the holes had been dug. Just to make the excavation a little deeper and line it with stones. That was the biggest part of the job. It is beautifully done too. Very regular. I wonder he took such pains when it was never to be seen in daylight."

"It looks like the inside of a well, except that they are more usually round."

"And much deeper. He would not have had *two* wells so close together either." The both stood staring at the contraption, trying to figure it out. DeVigne continued thinking aloud, "There was a lot of talk at one time, about ten years ago, of Bonaparte's invading England, you recall. This district was thought to be the likeliest point for invasion. Many of the families hereabouts had spots arranged to hide their valuables. I wouldn't be surprised if Andrew intended hiding the jewelry and plate and so on in these holes. That would have been just after his marriage, when there was still plenty to hide."

While they talked, Bobbie had to scramble into the hole and claim it for her own. The footmen, not satisfied with one miracle a day, were busily winding the chain around the other tree and heaving it, too, out of the earth. Bobbie climbed out of the first hole only to hurl herself into the other. Her stepmother, regarding the streaks of dirt on her pelisse, hadn't the heart to restrain her. She felt the urge to jump into the hole herself. Before many seconds, deVigne found an excuse to do just that, saying he'd help Bobbie get out, but once down in the excavation, he was in no hurry to get out, and began poking around the corners.

"Look, Mama, I found a bag!" Bobbie called up. In her fingers she held one of the canvas bags, which was well known by now to hold a hundred guineas.

"Oh, no, not again!" Mrs Grayshott cried in vexation.

DeVigne took the bag from the child and lifted her up onto the ground before clambering out himself. "Shall we rob your favorite charity of this one?" he asked Delsie.

"No, I shan't keep it."

"The boys deserve a bonus for their work. You have twenty-five hundred to give to the purse-pinched schoolteachers — a nice round figure. Let us share the wealth. We will include their labor in filling in the holes."

"Yes, a reward for stopping criminals is not uncommon," she allowed.

Watling nearly expired with self-importance when he was given the responsibility of passing out the reward, one guinea at a time, with a reminder at each coin that it was not to be wasted.

"Really, those stone-lined holes are so neatly done, it seems a shame to destroy them," Delsie said. "Perhaps some flowerpots . . ."

"Too much shade," he advised. "And leaving the trees as they are would be an invitation to the smugglers to return. If I did not stand so deep in disgrace already, I would dare to suggest you have the holes filled in at once and take the boxes off the tree roots to allow them to grow more normally." When she did not take him to task for this interference, he continued. "As I *am* in your black books, however, I will leave your common sense to recommend it to you."

"I suppose you are right, but it seems a pity."

Watling was sent off to the Hall at once for shovels, before she should change her mind. The three family members went to the Cottage, but they could not long keep their news to themselves. They had to pile into the carriage to run over to the Dower House to tell Lady Jane and Sir Harold the news.

250

"Ah, he was using those holes he had dug under the apple trees, was he?" Harold asked. "I should have known it. I recall his having it done at the time of the Bonaparte scare. It quite slipped my mind."

His wife turned a fulminating eye on him. "Do you mean to stand there and tell us, Harold, that you *knew* of those holes under the apple trees all this while, and didn't bother to tell us?"

"Of course I knew it. It was no secret."

"It was a secret from *us*," Jane snapped. "*You* did not know it, did you, Max?"

"Certainly not."

"I believe you was in London when he had it done," Harold said vaguely. "Used a design I showed him of an old Roman *impluvium*, and figured after the scare was over, he'd use them for that again."

"What the devil is an *impluvium*?" Jane asked irritably.

She heard in great detail, supported with sketches from various books, that an *impluvium* was a shallow rock-lined pool for catching rainwater in the days of the Roman occupation, and also used sometimes for ornamental purposes, such as decorative fish and lily pads, or for children to wade in.

"I want a wading pond!" Bobbie said at once.

"*I* should like an ornamental fish pond," her mama took it up. "DeVigne, could you not stop the men before they fill in our holes? If they are left perfectly open and visible, the smugglers would not use them."

"They're your holes," he capitulated, and together Bobbie, Delsie and deVigne dashed back to the

Cottage. Lady Jane and Sir Harold were not far behind them, to view the *impluvia* for themselves.

There was no danger that the work had already been done. A sort of informal holiday had been declared at both the Hall and the Dower House, with every maid and footman who could possibly evade his duties there to see Watling command his crew in the interesting feat of lifting the trees. As the employers were unaware of this holiday, however, the observers drifted off rather quickly.

"I knew I could smell brandy in this orchard," Jane declared, sniffing the air.

"What you was smelling was decaying apples," her husband pointed out. "They ferment, my dear. You recall we often have a grouse or pheasant drunk from eating, then fly against the windows and break his neck."

"Yes, and you will have fish drunk from the remains of brandy swimming into the walls of your hole and breaking their necks," Jane said, to show she was not convinced of any error on her part. "If they *have* necks."

"Fish do not have necks," Sir Harold informed her, and was summarily cut off when he proceeded to tell her what they did have. The morning was spent in examining the secret hiding place, and as Mrs Grayshott had no servants at all, the party repaired to the Hall for luncheon.

"Have you thought of what you will do with the money?" Harold asked Delsie.

"It will be used for some charitable purpose," she answered.

252

"Oxford could use it," he suggested. "You might set up a bursary in Andrew's name, or buy the Tatford Library Collection that is going up for auction."

"I like the idea of a bursary," she said, considering. "To help some poor but bright student further his education. Andrew was a Cambridge man. It ought to go to Cambridge, not Oxford."

"I daresay you could get the Tatford Library for twenty-five hundred," Sir Harold persisted.

"I wonder if Cambridge would rather have that than a bursary," was her highly unsatisfactory reply.

"Cambridge? What would Cambridge want with a classical library? Oxford is the place to study the classics," he said.

"Then I shall make it a bursary," she decided, appearing not to notice that his aim was to secure the money for his own school. "The Andrew Grayshott Memorial Bursary, it will be called."

Sir Harold opened his mouth to object, but was interrupted by his wife, who suggested "the Brandy Bursary" would be a suitable nickname. Discussion then turned on providing Mrs Grayshott with some temporary help till she managed to hire servants, and deVigne offered the resumption of Nellie's and Olive's services.

"I'll send a footman over so you have a man about the house," Jane added.

With this settled, it was time for the Grayshotts to go home. Miss Milne and Bobbie were called, and Jane and Harold went back to the Dower House.

As the carriage wended its familiar way down the lane to the post road, Delsie said to her stepdaughter, "Are you happy to be coming home at last?"

"Yes, but I'll like it better when we're all living together at the Hall. Uncle Max has five kittens in the barn."

Max cleared his throat, and ran a finger around his collar.

"What do you mean? We are not moving to the Hall," Delsie said to her daughter.

"Uncle Max says we are. Didn't you, Uncle Max?"

"That is not exactly what I said," he parried.

With a barely concealed smile, Miss Milne said that perhaps Lord deVigne would give Bobbie one of his kittens.

"I don't want one. I want them all," she replied.

"Precocious. You are turning into a woman already," her uncle complimented her.

At the Cottage, Miss Milne took her charge upstairs, and Mrs Grayshott at once rounded on deVigne. "You know I promised Andrew faithfully *I* would look after Roberta. I hope you have not been giving her the idea she is to go to *you*. I don't know how you think I should allow it, when the main reason I married Andrew was to provide a guardian for her."

"You were not listening very carefully. What she said was that *we* would all be living together at the Hall."

Having a very good inkling as to his meaning, the widow blushed up to her eyes, and pointed out that such a scheme was entirely ineligible, for a widow in no way related to him to be moving into a bachelor's establishment.

"That is true, and we would have to arrange some relationship," he answered reasonably.

"There is no way it could be arranged."

"One suffers to think of a schoolteacher having so little use of her wits. It could be arranged very easily by our marrying."

"You would do *anything* to get hold of Roberta!" she accused him.

"Yes, I am quite determined to get my clutches on *Roberta*!" he agreed, smiling. "I am resigned to having that charge thrown at my head every time you feel out of sorts, which happens remarkably often, by the by. But so long as we both know it is merely a stick to beat me with, I am willing to accept it."

"I wonder at your lack of propriety! Andrew scarcely cold in his grave —"

"He must be cooled down considerably. It is December, after all."

"I was speaking metaphorically."

"That's what I get for making up to a schoolmistress. How long must we wait?"

"Till hell freezes over."

"That should cool him down all right. Do you mean we must wait out the whole year?"

"I meant nothing of the sort!"

"Good, I think six months more than enough myself."

"You know I didn't mean that."

"I am ravished at your eagerness, but really we ought to wait till you are at least in half mourning, don't you think?"

"You are being purposely obtuse. I can't possibly marry you! Two marriages in one year. It is monstrous."

"True, but it is already December, and will soon be next year. We'll consign your nominal marriage to Andrew to this year, and —"

"Yes, I see what you are about. Trying to rush me into it again, before I have time to think. Don't forget to point out all the advantages that will accrue me. A domineering, mulish husband who doesn't even stick at drugging, and kidnapping me, a vastly superior home, a title —"

"You're doing a pretty good job of convincing yourself. Only think, never again to be called by the odious name of Mrs Grayshott. That must bear heavily on the side of the advantages."

"We would be laughing stocks in the village," she objected weakly, and looked hopefully to him for refutation.

"They could well do with a few laughs in Questnow. Things are remarkably flat in the winter. Of course it bothers *me* enormously what Mr Umpton and Miss Frisk think, and I'm sure you too shrink from doing anything they would dislike."

"It would almost be worth putting up with you to see Umpton stare."

"No price is too high to pay for that sort of a treat. We'll call on him together, and both watch him stare," he answered gravely, his lips only a little unsteady.

256

"I said *almost* worth it. Jane warned me — not that you haven't *already* locked me up in a room and beat me."

"No, no, not *beat*! Be fair. A crack on the skull is not a beating. I save that for after the wedding. Or were you speaking metaphorically again, referring to my having *bested* you in the matter of rooting you out of the Cottage last night?"

"You cheated anyway."

"I took a slightly unfair advantage." He advanced toward her and removed the driving cape from her shoulders, tossing it on a chair. "I don't mean to do so again, Delsie," he said, looking at her intently, with all the levity gone from his voice. "I was horrified when I saw what I had done to you last night. Indeed, ever since this smuggling business reared its ugly head I have regretted dragging you into it." He touched the plaster on her forehead, and ran one finger slowly down her cheek. "Can you forgive me for that?"

"It was an accident. I know you didn't do it on purpose."

"But I *did* it, and I shan't forgive myself. I was afraid I'd hurt you badly —"

"Don't be ridiculous — a mere bump on the head," she laughed unsteadily.

"You are generous, but I vowed I would make it up to you."

"Is *that* why you are offering for me?" she demanded.

"You are foolish beyond belief," he said angrily, and pulled her into his arms. "I am marrying you because I don't want you to leave us, ever. Because I have never been so happy as since you came to us. Because I love you, Delsie Sommers." He looked hard at her face for a few seconds, then closed his eyes and kissed her. When he released her several moments later, he added, "And I am conceited enough to think half your fits of pique are due to loving me, despite your own better judgment."

"I am not really Delsie Sommers any more," she answered dreamily.

"You *are, really*," he disagreed firmly, and bent his head to kiss her again.

They were interrupted by the sound of feet thumping on the stairs and Bobbie came into the room. "I heard somebody coming," she said.

"Your hearing is definitely impaired," deVigne told her, displeased at her arrival.

"No, it isn't. I hear very good."

"Very well," Delsie corrected automatically.

"See, Mama says so too. But you want to get rid of me so you can be alone with Mama. I heard Sally say at the Hall you're always running to Mama." On this remark she ran to the door.

"I have been found out," he informed Delsie. "Even the servants and a child see through me. 'Always running to Mama'."

"She shouldn't be gossiping with the servants."

"Only eavesdropping. Sharp as a tack, our Bobbie."

It was soon clear her hearing was also sharp. There had been a cart driven up outside, unheard by the two in the saloon, who were so happily occupied otherwise. It was Delsie's ex-students, come to inquire whether

Mrs Grayshott still wanted their services. These were gratefully accepted, and it was arranged for the girls to return the next morning with their belongings to take up work at the Cottage.

"Word must be out that we no longer run a smuggling den here," deVigne said.

"How flat it will be, with no pixies in the garden and no bags of gold regularly deposited under the tree."

"We shall do our poor best to keep you entertained, Miss Sommers."

"Mrs Grayshott."

"How strange, now that you are about to be rid of the name, you develop this inexplicable passion for it. I wish to forget I ever cajoled you into marrying Andrew. Though I suppose otherwise I should never have come to know you. I had no suspicion, to see you in the village, that we should suit in the least. A regular little nun, I thought. Jane is wiser. Nonesuch, she said, and she was right."

"Lady Jane will not be happy with this business. She has picked out a Miss Haversham for your wife, and I hope she will not be too disappointed at your refusing to have her."

"Miss Haversham?" he asked, frowning. "She is sixty-five, give or take a decade."

"No, no. It must be a different Miss Haversham, a younger one."

"The younger one is sixty-five; she has an elder sister eighty or so. Where did you get this idea?"

"She told me."

"The old terror!" he exclaimed, laughing. "She has been trying to make you jealous. Observing my penchant for your company, as did the servants, she wanted to give you a nudge."

"The sly creature! Let us not tell her we are to be married, and watch her finagle."

The secret lasted less than halfway through dinner that evening. Jane first observed that the two had dispensed with formal names and titles and were on a first-name basis. When deVigne inadvertently mentioned, during a discussion of hiring a housekeeper, that her services would be very temporary and Mrs Lambton would be good enough for a few months, she was onto them, but kept up the game.

"A few months? Oh, she is young enough to last a few *years*, Max."

"I meant years," he said, with a conscious look at Delsie, who smiled sheepishly.

"Of course you did," Lady Jane smiled knowingly. "Why should Delsie only require her services for six months, till she is out of deep mourning? Dear me, there could be no reason. None in the world. It is not as though she will be leaving the Cottage."

"Certainly not," Sir Harold added foolishly, the only one at the table who had not perceived what was going on before his eyes. His wife turned a withering look on him.

"For, of course, you will not be *leaving* us," Jane continued, her irony becoming stronger by the moment.

"Oh, no," Delsie agreed.

"Or moving to the Hall," Jane said at last, with a piercing observation of the pair of culprits.

"Miss Haversham would not care for that," Delsie answered her with an innocent smile.

"Miss Haversham?" Harold asked in confusion. "Why, what is it to *her*? Nosy old biddy. As to moving to the Hall, it is out of the question, of course. Quite out of the question. Not the thing at all."

"Harold, you ninny," Jane said baldly. "They are to be married!"

"*Who* is to be married?" he demanded in vexation. "Miss Havershamn is too old to marry anyone. Old as the stars. Older."

"Not her, Max and Delsie," Jane explained.

"Eh? Both of them? Who are they marrying?"

"Each other, Harold," Jane told him patiently.

"Really? Marrying each other, you say? Well, bless my soul. When did all this come about?"

"Why, I wouldn't be surprised if it was about the same time Max started flirting with Miss Haversham," Jane said with smug satisfaction at her scheme's success.

"*Her* again!" Sir Harold fumed. "Max, you haven't set up a flirtation with that old Tartar. Old enough to be your grandmother, 'pon my word. I don't know what this world is coming to. Louise marrying that old slice of a Grayshott, then Delsie marrying him, and now Delsie marrying Max, after he's taken to throwing his cap at Miss Haversham."

Their incredulous smiles made even Sir Harold aware that he had been conned, and he laughed at himself. "All a hum, I dare say," he said, and ate up his soup.

Later, Jane shooed him off to the library to be rid of him while quizzing the two about their plans. When she had discovered what she wished to know, she cautioned them to leave before he came out, or he'd make them listen to his translation of Pliny, when she was sure they had more interesting things to talk about. "Not that you'll get much *talking* done, I warrant," she added roguishly.

Nor did they. Still, they managed to set on June thirtieth for a wedding day, and to agree on a locale for the honeymoon, as Delsie had been gypped out of one the first time around. The young lady was consulted so punctiliously on every point that it was necessary for her to remind her fiancé she had put him in charge of all details of her second wedding before she had contracted her first.

"Since I am in charge of all details," he said slyly, "I think the bride must have a few lessons in what her groom will like."

"Several large doses of brandy a day, like her first husband, I collect," she replied.

"That, of course, and several large doses of love a night. *Unlike* her first husband." His arm, already around her waist in the carriage, tightened as he pulled her to him. "Time for my first medication."

"I have ended up a nurse after all," she sighed, and administered a light peck to his cheek.

"A very stingy nurse! Several large doses was the prescription," he reminded her, then proceeded to fill the prescription. "More addicting than brandy," he murmured.

"You will please to stay sober till June thirtieth, milord."

"So I shall, but on June thirtieth, Delsie Sommers, I intend to become roaring drunk."

"I intend to become a little foxed myself on that day," she promised happily.

Also available in ISIS Large Print:

The Duke & I

Julia Quinn

After enduring two seasons in London, Daphne Bridgerton is no longer naïve enough to believe she will be able to marry for love. But is it really too much to hope for a husband for whom she at least has some affection?

Her brother's old school friend Simon Bassett — the new Duke of Hastings — has no intention of ever marrying. However, newly returned to England, he finds himself the target of the many society mothers who remain convinced that reformed rakes make the best husbands.

To deflect their attention, the handsome hell-raiser proposes to Daphne that they pretend an attachment. In return, his interest in Daphne will ensure she becomes the belle of London society with suitors beating a path to her door . . .

There's just one problem, Daphne is now in danger of falling for a man who has no intention of making their charade a reality . . .

ISBN 978-0-7531-8040-2 (hb)
ISBN 978-0-7531-8041-9 (pb)

The River Knows

Amanda Quick

The first kiss occurred in a dimly-lit hallway on the upper floor of Elwin Hasting's grand house. Louisa never saw it coming . . .

Of course, Anthony Stalbridge couldn't possibly have had romantic intentions. The kiss was meant to distract the armed guard. After all, Louisa Bryce is no man's idea of an alluring female. The only thing they have in common is a passionate interest in the private affairs of Mr Hastings — a prominent member of Victorian Society whom they both suspect of hiding terrible secrets.

Each has a reason for the quest. Anthony has suspicions about the death of his fiancée. Louisa — whose identity is shrouded in layers of mystery — is convinced Hastings has a connection to a notorious brothel.

But bringing Hastings to justice will be more perilous than either anticipates — and their hasty partnership will be more heated than either expects.

ISBN 978-0-7531-7974-1 (hb)
ISBN 978-0-7531-7975-8 (pb)

Searching for Tilly

Susan Sallis

A touching story of love, loss and discovery.

Three women came to the remote Cornish cottage that summer: Jenna, only 26 and grieving for the loss of the love of her life; her mother Caro, whose husband Steve had also died; and Laura, who had been married to Caro's beloved brother Geoff. The house where they were staying was called The Widow's Cottage, and it was poignantly suitable.

In that tiny Cornish community, the three discover strange memories of their forebears, and especially of Tilly, Cora's mother. They become swept up in the story of Tilly and her family — a story that takes them on an epic journey across the West Country and to the solution of an amazing family mystery.

ISBN 978-0-7531-7952-9 (hb)
ISBN 978-0-7531-7953-6 (pb)

Peter West

D. E. Stevenson

Beth Kerr is the daughter of the boatman in the small village of Kintoul. Her mother died at an early age, after an unhappy marriage that caused her family to cast her aside. As the years pass, Beth grows into a beautiful young woman, watched over by the quiet Peter West. The owner of Kintoul House, Peter is a lonely man with a weak heart and few family members and friends. They both struggle with their feelings for one another, before being forced to embark on marriages decided upon by their families. But will their lives follow the paths set for them, or will they find their own way?

ISBN 978-0-7531-7824-9 (hb)
ISBN 978-0-7531-7825-6 (pb)